MODERN SHORT STORIES TWO

MODERN
SHORT STORIES
TWO

★

*edited with an introduction
and notes by*

JIM HUNTER

faber and faber
LONDON · BOSTON

First published in 1994
by Faber and Faber Limited
3 Queen Square London WC1N 3AU

Typeset by Datix International Limited, Bungay, Suffolk
Printed in England by Clays Ltd, St Ives plc

A CIP record for this book is available
from the British Library

ISBN 0-571-16986-4

2 4 6 8 10 9 7 5 3 1

CONTENTS

★

INTRODUCTION

★

All the stories here were first written for adult readers, and I hope the book makes a good read for anyone. The collection is designed, however, for educational use, with students from age 14 upwards. The material gets more demanding as the book goes on.

There is a lot of laughter here, but little or no triviality. These are strong stories, about fundamental human experiences: to me that is the foremost educational value of the collection. But the notes also offer some training in literary study, by gradually acclimatizing the reader to discussion of five main elements of fiction: plot, character, setting, style and viewpoint. Of course these can be hard to separate (for example, 'character', 'style' and 'viewpoint' in some first-person narrations); and the notes on any one story rarely mention more than two or three of the five elements. But such structure can be helpful in firming up early vague reactions and in suggesting further enquiry. At the end of the book are some suggestions and questions for comparative study between stories.

Ideally many of these stories will first be heard read aloud. The days when families read Dickens' novels to each other have long gone, but the short story is still ideal for this kind of sharing. There is some overlap with drama: the tension or compassion or amusement is a shared artistic experience and tends to dig emotionally much deeper than a silent solo reading. The reading aloud should be by one good reader who knows the story in advance (in schools and colleges, usually the teacher). In some cases (e.g. 'The Bewitched Jacket', or 'Telling Stories' or 'Maria') the reader can pause before the final section and invite listeners to devise their own endings.

This new collection of mostly recent fiction is published as a companion to *Modern Short Stories One*, which has already been widely used for many years.

JIM HUNTER

DINO BUZZATI

The Italian poet and fiction-writer Dino Buzzati lived from
1906 to 1972. Like several of his other stories, 'The Bewitched
Jacket' may remind us of ancient tales of the supernatural
though it is set in a modern city. Greed and guilt and fear are
timeless emotions.

The Bewitched Jacket

Although I appreciate elegant dress, I don't usually pay
attention to the perfection (or imperfection) with which my
companions' clothing is cut.

None the less, one night during a reception at a house in
Milan, I met a man about forty years old who literally shone
because of the simple and decisive beauty of his clothes.

I don't know who he was, I was meeting him for the first
time, and at the introduction, as always happens, it was
impossible to get his name. But at a certain point during the
evening, I found myself near him, and we began to talk. He
seemed a civil, well-bred man, but with an air of sadness.
Perhaps with exaggerated familiarity – God should have
stopped me – I complimented him on his elegance; and I even
dared to ask him who his tailor might be.

He smiled curiously, as if he had expected my question.
'Nearly no one knows him,' he said. 'Still, he's a great

1

master. And he works only when it comes to him. For a few initiates.'

'So that I couldn't . . .?'

'Oh, try, try. His name is Corticella, Alfonso Corticella, via Ferrara 17.'

'He will be expensive, I imagine.'

'I believe so, but I swear I don't know. He made me this suit three years ago, and he still hasn't sent me the bill.'

'Corticella? Via Ferrara 17, did you say?'

'Exactly,' the stranger answered. And he left me to join another group of people.

At via Ferrara 17, I found a house like so many others and like those of so many other tailors; it was the residence of Alfonso Corticella. It was he who came to let me in. He was a little old man with black hair, which was, however, obviously dyed.

To my surprise, he was not hard to deal with. In fact, he seemed eager for me to be his customer. I explained to him how I had got his address, praised his cutting, and asked him to make me a suit. We selected a grey wool, then he took my measurements, and offered to come to my apartment for the fitting. I asked him the price. There was no hurry, he answered, we could always come to an agreement. What a congenial man, I thought at first. Nevertheless, later, while I was returning home, I realized that the little old man had left me feeling uneasy (perhaps because of his much too warm and persistent smiles). In short, I had no desire at all to see him again. But now the suit had been ordered. And after about three weeks it was ready.

When they brought it to me, I tried it on in front of a mirror for a little while. It was a masterpiece. Yet, I don't know why, perhaps because of my memory of the unpleasant old man, I didn't have any desire to wear it. And weeks passed before I decided to do so.

2

That day I shall remember forever. It was a Tuesday in April and it was raining. When I had slipped into the clothes – jacket, trousers, and vest – I was pleased to observe that they didn't pull and weren't tight anywhere, as almost always happens with new suits. And yet they wrapped me perfectly.

As a rule I put nothing in the right jacket pocket; in the left one, I keep my cards. This explains why, only after a couple of hours at the office, casually slipping my hand into the right pocket, I noticed that there was a piece of paper inside. Was it maybe the tailor's bill?

No. It was a ten thousand lire note.

I was astounded. I certainly had not put it there. On the other hand, it was absurd to think it a joke of the tailor Corticella. Much less did it seem a gift from my maid, the only person, other than the tailor, who had occasion to go near my suit. Or was it a counterfeit note? I looked at it in the light, I compared it to other ones. It couldn't be any better than these.

There was a single possible explanation: Corticella's absent-mindedness. Perhaps a customer had come to make a payment. The tailor didn't have his wallet with him just then, and so to avoid leaving the money around, he slipped it into my jacket, which was hanging on a mannequin. These things can happen.

I rang for my secretary. I wanted to write a letter to Corticella, returning the money that was not mine. Yet (and I can't say why I did it) I slipped my hand into the pocket again.

'Is anything wrong, sir? Do you feel ill?' asked my secretary, who entered at that moment. I must have turned pale as death. In my pocket my fingers touched the edge of another strip of paper – which had not been there a few minutes before.

'No, no, it's nothing,' I said. 'A slight dizziness. It happens

3

to me sometimes. Maybe I'm a little tired. You can go now, dear, I wanted to dictate a letter, but we'll do it later.'

Only after my secretary had gone did I dare remove the piece of paper from my pocket. It was another ten thousand lire note. Then I tried a third time. And a third banknote came out.

My heart began to race. I had the feeling that for some mysterious reason I was involved in the plot of a fairy tale, like those that are told to children and that no one believes are true.

On the pretext that I was not feeling well, I left the office and went home. I needed to be alone. Luckily, my maid had already gone. I shut the doors, lowered the blinds. I began to take out the notes one after another, very quickly. My pocket seemed inexhaustible.

I worked in a spasmodic nervous tension, with the fear that the miracle might stop at any moment. I wanted it to continue all day and night, until I had accumulated billions. But at a certain point the flow diminished.

Before me stood an impressive heap of banknotes. The important thing now was to hide them, so no one might get wind of the affair. I emptied an old trunk full of rugs and put the money, arranged in many little piles, at the bottom. Then I slowly began counting. There were 58 million lire.

I awoke the next morning after the maid arrived. She was amazed to find me in bed still completely dressed. I tried to laugh, explaining that I had drunk a little too much the night before and sleep had suddenly seized me.

A new anxiety arose: she asked me to take off the suit, so she could at least give it a brushing.

I answered that I had to go out immediately and didn't have time to change. Then I hurried to a store selling ready-to-wear clothes to buy another suit made of a similar material; I would leave this one in the maid's care; 'mine', the suit that in the course of a few days would make me one of the most powerful men in the world, I would hide in a safe place.

4

I didn't know whether I was living in a dream, whether I was happy or rather suffocating under the burden of too hard a fate. On the street, I was continually feeling the magic pocket through my raincoat. Each time I breathed a sigh of relief. Beneath the cloth answered the comforting crackle of paper money

But a singular coincidence cooled my joyous delirium. News of a robbery that occurred the day before headlined the morning papers. A bank's armoured car, after making the rounds of the branches, was carrying the day's deposits to the main office when it was seized and cleaned out in viale Palmanova by four criminals. As people swarmed around the scene, one of the gangsters began to shoot to keep them away. A passerby was killed. But, above all, the amount of the loot struck me: it was exactly 58 million – like the money I had put in the trunk.

Could there be a connection between my sudden wealth and the criminal raid that happened almost simultaneously? It seemed foolish to think so. What's more, I am not superstitious. All the same, the incident left me very confused.

The more one gets, the more one wants. I was already rich, considering my modest habits. But the illusion of a life of unlimited luxury was compelling. And that same evening I set to work again. Now I proceeded more slowly, with less torture to my nerves. Another 135 million was added to my previous treasure.

That night I couldn't close my eyes. Was it the presentiment of danger? Or the tormented conscience of one who undeservedly wins a fabulous fortune? Or was it a kind of confused remorse? At dawn I leaped from the bed, dressed, and ran outside to get a newspaper.

As I read, I lost my breath. A terrible fire, which had begun in a naphtha warehouse, had half-destroyed a building on the main street, via San Cloro. The flames had consumed, among other things, the safes of a large real estate company which contained more than 130 million in cash. Two firemen met their deaths in the blaze.

Should I now, perhaps, list my crimes one by one? Yes, because now I knew that the money the jacket gave me came from those crimes, from blood, from desperation and death, from hell. But I was still within the snare of reason, which scornfully refused to admit that I was in any way responsible. And then the temptation resumed, then the hand – it was so easy! – slipped into the pocket, and the fingers, with the quickest delight, grasped the edges of always another bank-note. The money, the divine money!

Without moving out of my old apartment (so as not to attract attention), I soon bought a huge villa, owned a precious collection of paintings, drove around in luxurious automobiles, and having left my firm for 'reasons of health', travelled back and forth throughout the world in the company of marvellous women.

I knew that whenever I drew money from the jacket, something base and painful happened in the world. But it was still always a vague awareness, not supported by logical proofs. Meanwhile, at each new collection, my conscience was degraded, becoming more and more vile. And the tailor? I telephoned him to ask for the bill, but no one answered. In via Ferrara, where I went to search for him, they told me that he had emigrated abroad, they didn't know where. Everything then conspired to show me that without knowing it, I was bound in a pact with the Devil.

Until one morning, in the building where I lived for many years, they found a sixty-year-old retired woman asphyxiated by gas; she had killed herself for having mislaid her monthly pension of 30 thousand lire, which she had collected the day before (and which had ended up in my hands).

Enough, enough! In order not to sink to the depths of the abyss, I had to rid myself of the jacket. And not by surrendering it to someone else, because the horror would continue (who would ever be able to resist such enticement?). Its destruction was absolutely necessary.

By car I arrived at a secluded valley in the Alps. I left the car in a grassy clearing and set out in the direction of the forest. There wasn't a living soul in sight. Having gone beyond the forest, I reached the rocky ground of the moraine. Here, between two gigantic boulders, I pulled the wicked jacket from the knapsack, sprinkled it with kerosene, and lit it. In a few minutes only ashes were left.

But at the last flicker of the flames, behind me – it seemed about two or three metres away – a human voice resounded: 'Too late, too late!' Terrified, I turned around with a serpent's snap. But I saw no one. I explored the area, jumping from one huge rock to another, to hunt out the damned person. Nothing. There were only rocks.

Notwithstanding the fright I experienced, I went back down to the base of the valley with a feeling of relief. I was free at last. And rich, luckily.

But my car was no longer in the grassy clearing. And after I returned to the city, my sumptuous villa had disappeared; in its place was an uncultivated field with some poles that bore the notice 'Municipal Land For Sale'. My savings accounts were also completely drained, but I couldn't explain how. The big packets of deeds in my numerous safe-deposit boxes had vanished too. And there was dust, nothing but dust, in the old trunk.

I now resumed working with difficulty, I hardly get through a day, and what is stranger, no one seems to be amazed by my sudden ruin.

And I know that it's still not over, I know that one day my

doorbell will ring, I'll answer it and find that cursed tailor before me, with his contemptible smile, asking for the final settling of my account.

Many writers want to bring the power of classical or medieval legend to their own times. 'The Bewitched Jacket' is a moral fable, traditional in its mentions of God and the Devil, but modern in its recognition that one person's wealth may depend on other people's suffering.

What other stories, or real-life situations, does it remind you of? Can you make up a similar modern-day fable of your own?

The plot of a story is the way its events hang together. The word doesn't necessarily imply something cunning or secret: a story may be quite open and straightforward, and we still talk of its plot, meaning its basic chain of events. But in the best plots things are so linked as to press one event on into the next: it's not just that C chances to follow A and B, but that the combination of A and B requires C to happen. Once the narrator (the person telling us the story, in this case also the main character) discovers that every time he draws money out of the jacket someone else suffers correspondingly, he is locked into a situation which has to be resolved – if he has any human feeling at all.

Some plots play on our dreams; some on our nightmares. A few very special ones, such as this, play on both at once.

The viewpoint is that of the central character. Yet we learn little about him: he likes women and cars and wealth, but those aren't exactly unusual tastes. Not all stories depend on strong drawing of character: event and situation may be much more important. Here the undefined characterization may allow each of us individually to identify with the narrator – which is part of the story's function as a fable.

DOROTHY PARKER

★

Dorothy Parker (1893–1967) grew up and died in New York, though part of her life was spent writing for film studios in California. She wrote poems, stories and reviews, and was also famous for her fiercely witty conversation – today, she would certainly have been on the international TV chat-show circuit.

Like many humorists, Dorothy Parker was in some respects a sad person. And she felt strongly about serious matters, such as the way women, or black people, were treated by American society in her day. (In her will she left everything to the National Association for the Advancement of Colored People.)

A Telephone Call

———————————— ★ ————————————

Please, God, let him telephone me now. Dear God, let him call me now. I won't ask anything else of You, truly I won't. It isn't very much to ask. It would be so little to You, God, such a little, little thing. Only let him telephone now. Please, God. Please, please, please.

If I didn't think about it, maybe the telephone might ring. Sometimes it does that. If I could think of something else. If I could think of something else. Maybe if I counted five hundred by fives, it might ring by that time. I'll count slowly. I won't cheat. And if it rings when I get to three hundred, I won't stop; I won't answer it until I get to five hundred. Five, ten, fifteen, twenty, twenty-five, thirty, thirty-five, forty, forty-five, fifty. . . . Oh, please ring. Please.

This is the last time I'll look at the clock. I will not look at it again. It's ten minutes past seven. He said he would telephone at five o'clock. 'I'll call you at five, darling.' I think that's where he said 'darling'. I'm almost sure he said it there. I know he called me 'darling' twice, and the other time was when he said goodbye. 'Goodbye, darling.' He was busy, and he can't say much in the office, but he called me 'darling' twice. He couldn't have minded my calling him up. I know you shouldn't keep telephoning them – I know they don't like that. When you do that, they know you are thinking about them and wanting them, and that makes them hate you. But I hadn't talked to him in three days – not in three days. And all I did was ask him how he was; it was just the way anybody might have called him up. He couldn't have minded that. He couldn't have thought I was bothering him. 'No, of course you're not,' he said. And he said he'd telephone me. He didn't have to say that. I didn't ask him to, truly I didn't. I'm sure I didn't. I don't think he would say he'd telephone me, and then just never do it. Please don't let him do that. God. Please don't.

'I'll call you at five, darling.' 'Goodbye, darling.' He was busy, and he was in a hurry, and there were people around him, but he called me 'darling' twice. That's mine, that's mine. I have that, even if I never see him again. Oh, but that's so little. That isn't enough. Nothing's enough, if I never see him again. Please let me see him again, God. Please, I want him so much. I want him so much. I'll be good, God. I will try to be better, I will, if You will let me see him again. If You let him telephone me. Oh, let him telephone me now.

Ah, don't let my prayer seem too little to You, God. You

sit up there, so white and old, with all the angels about You and the stars slipping by. And I come to You with a prayer about a telephone call. Ah, don't laugh, God. You see, You don't know how it feels. You're so safe, there on Your throne, with the blue swirling under You. Nothing can touch You; no one can twist Your heart in his hands. This is suffering, God, this is bad, bad suffering. Won't You help me? For Your Son's sake, help me. You said You would do whatever was asked of You in His name. Oh, God, in the name of Thine only beloved Son, Jesus Christ, our Lord, let him telephone me now.

I must stop this. I mustn't be this way. Look. Suppose a young man says he'll call a girl up, and then something happens, and he doesn't. That isn't so terrible, is it? Why, it's going on all over the world, right this minute. Oh, what do I care what's going on all over the world? Why can't that telephone ring? Why can't it, why can't it? Couldn't you ring? Ah, please, couldn't you? You damned, ugly, shiny thing. It would hurt you to ring, wouldn't it? Oh, that would hurt you. Damn you, I'll pull your filthy roots out of the wall, I'll smash your smug black face in little bits. Damn you to hell.

No, no, no. I must stop. I must think about something else. This is what I'll do. I'll put the clock in the other room. Then I can't look at it. If I do have to look at it, then I'll have to walk into the bedroom, and that will be something to do. Maybe, before I look at it again, he will call me. I'll be so sweet to him, if he calls me. If he says he can't see me tonight, I'll say, 'Why, that's all right, dear. Why, of course it's all right.' I'll be the way I was when I first met him. Then maybe he'll like me again. I was always sweet, at first. Oh, it's so easy to be sweet to people before you love them.

I think he must still like me a little. He couldn't have called me 'darling' twice today, if he didn't still like me a little. It isn't all gone, if he still likes me a little; even if it's only a little, little bit. You see, God, if You would just let him telephone me, I wouldn't have to ask You anything more. I would be sweet to him, I would be gay, I would be just the way I used to be, and then he would love me again. And then I would never have to ask You for anything more. Don't You see, God? So won't You please let him telephone me? Won't You please, please, please?

Are You punishing me, God, because I've been bad? Are You angry with me because I did that? Oh, but, God, there are so many bad people – You could not be hard only to me. And it wasn't very bad; it couldn't have been bad. We didn't hurt anybody, God. Things are only bad when they hurt people. We didn't hurt one single soul; You know that. You know it wasn't bad, don't You, God? So won't You let him telephone me now?

If he doesn't telephone me, I'll know God is angry with me. I'll count five hundred by fives, and if he hasn't called me then, I will know God isn't going to help me, ever again. That will be the sign. Five, ten, fifteen, twenty, twenty-five, thirty, thirty-five, forty, forty-five, fifty, fifty-five ... It was bad. I knew it was bad. All right, God, send me to hell. You think You're frightening me with Your hell, don't You? You think Your hell is worse than mine.

I mustn't. I mustn't do this. Suppose he's a little late calling me up – that's nothing to get hysterical about. Maybe he isn't going to call – maybe he's coming straight up here without telephoning. He'll be cross if he sees I have been crying. They don't like you to cry. He doesn't cry. I wish to God I could make him cry. I wish I could make him cry and tread the floor and feel his heart heavy and big and festering in him. I wish I could hurt him like hell.

He doesn't wish that about me. I don't think he even knows how he makes me feel. I wish he could know, without my telling him. They don't like you to tell them they've made

12

you cry. They don't like you to tell them you're unhappy because of them. If you do, they think you're possessive and exacting. And then they hate you. They hate you whenever you say anything you really think. You always have to keep playing little games. Oh, I thought we didn't have to; I thought this was so big I could say whatever I meant. I guess you can't, ever. I guess there isn't ever anything big enough for that. Oh, if he would just telephone, I wouldn't tell him I had been sad about him. They hate sad people. I would be so sweet and so gay, he couldn't help but like me. If he would only telephone. If he would only telephone.

Maybe that's what he is doing. Maybe he is coming on here without calling me up. Maybe he's on his way now. Something might have happened to him. No, nothing could ever happen to him. I can't picture anything happening to him. I never picture him run over. I never see him lying still and long and dead. I wish he were dead. That's a terrible wish. That's a lovely wish. If he were dead, he would be mine. If he were dead, I would never think of now and the last few weeks. I would remember only the lovely times. It would be all beautiful. I wish he were dead. I wish he were dead, dead, dead.

This is silly. It's silly to go wishing people were dead just because they don't call you up the very minute they said they would. Maybe the clock's fast; I don't know whether it's right. Maybe he's hardly late at all. Anything could have made him a little late. Maybe he had to stay at his office. Maybe he went home, to call me up from there, and somebody came in. He doesn't like to telephone me in front of people. Maybe he's worried, just a little, little bit, about keeping me waiting. He might even hope that I would call him up. I could do that. I could telephone him.

I mustn't. I mustn't. I mustn't. Oh, God, please don't let me telephone him. Please keep me from doing that. I know, God, just as well as You do, that if he were worried about me, he'd telephone no matter where he was or how many people there were around him. Please make me know that, God. I don't ask You to make it easy for me – You can't do that, for all that You could make a world. Only let me know it, God. Don't let me go on hoping. Don't let me say comforting things to myself. Please don't let me hope, dear God. Please don't.

I won't telephone him. I'll never telephone him again as long as I live. He'll rot in hell, before I'll call him up. You don't have to give me strength, God; I have it myself. If he wanted me, he could get me. He knows where I am. He knows I'm waiting here. He's so sure of me, so sure. I wonder why they hate you, as soon as they are sure of you. I should think it would be so sweet to be sure.

It would be so easy to telephone him. Then I'd know. Maybe it wouldn't be a foolish thing to do. Maybe he wouldn't mind. Maybe he'd like it. Maybe he has been trying to get me. Sometimes people try and try to get you on the telephone, and they say the number doesn't answer. I'm not just saying that to help myself; that really happens. You know that really happens, God. Oh, God, keep me away from that telephone. Keep me away. Let me still have just a little bit of pride. I think I'm going to need it, God. I think it will be all I'll have.

Oh, what does pride matter, when I can't stand it if I don't talk to him? Pride like that is such a silly, shabby little thing. The real pride, the big pride, is in having no pride. I'm not saying that just because I want to call him. I am not. That's true, I know that's true. I will be big. I will be beyond little prides.

Please, God, keep me from telephoning him. Please, God.

I don't see what pride has to do with it. This is such a little thing, for me to be bringing in pride, for me to be making such a fuss about. I may have misunderstood him. Maybe he

said for me to call him up, at five. 'Call me at five, darling.'
He could have said that, perfectly well. It's so possible that I
didn't hear him right. 'Call me at five, darling.' I'm almost
sure that's what he said. God, don't let me talk this way to
myself. Make me know, please make me know.

I'll think about something else. I'll just sit quietly. If I
could sit still. If I could sit still. Maybe I could read. Oh, all
the books are about people who love each other, truly and
sweetly. What do they want to write about that for? Don't
they know it isn't true? Don't they know it's a lie, it's a God
damned lie? What do they have to tell about that for, when
they know how it hurts? Damn them, damn them, damn
them.

I won't. I'll be quiet. This is nothing to get excited about.
Look. Suppose he were someone I didn't know very well.
Suppose he were another girl. Then I'd just telephone and
say, 'Well, for goodness' sake, what happened to you?' That's
what I'd do, and I'd never even think about it. Why can't I be
casual and natural, just because I love him? I can be. Hon-
estly. I can be. I'll call him up, and be so easy and pleasant.
You see if I won't, God. Oh, don't let me call him. Don't,
don't, don't.

God, aren't You really going to let him call me? Are You
sure, God? Couldn't You please relent? Couldn't You? I
don't even ask You to let him telephone me this minute,
God: only let him do it in a little while. I'll count five
hundred by fives. I'll do it so slowly and so fairly. If he hasn't
telephoned then, I'll call him. I will. Oh, please, dear God,
dear kind God, my blessed Father in Heaven, let him call
before then. Please, God. Please.

Five, ten, fifteen, twenty, twenty-five, thirty, thirty-five . . .

★

Here fiction and drama meet: though printed to be read, it is equally a script for performance. Try rehearsing it: that shows up the many shifts and changes as the speaker pleads and whines and wheedles with God.

This sequence of emotional events might be said to be the plot; and it stops before it's resolved. (Is she going to call him? What will be his reaction if she does?) But there is also a longer-term plot, off-stage: the history of her relationship with the man who isn't calling her. We can guess much of it: take, for example, the words 'if he still likes me a little'.

In a monologue like this, both plot and character are gradually revealed to us, without the speaker's intending it. We hear it all from her viewpoint; but she's in such a bad way that we may instinctively stand back from identifying with her too closely.

Is it a funny piece? Or a desperately sad one? Perhaps it can be both at once?

FOR FURTHER READING:

A fat collection called *The Penguin Dorothy Parker*. There, for example, can be found her two-line poem 'Men seldom make passes / At girls who wear glasses', or her review of A. A. Milne, over the pen-name of Constant Reader, which ends: 'And it is that word "hummy", my darlings, that marks the first place in *A House at Pooh Corner* at which Tonstant Weader Fwowed up.'

MAEVE BINCHY

Maeve Binchy was born in Dublin and has worked as a teacher and journalist. She is well known for her novels and short stories.

Telling Stories

People always said that Irene had total recall. She seemed to remember the smallest details of things they had long forgotten – the words of old pop songs, the shades of old lipsticks, minute-by-minute reconstructions of important events like Graduation Day, or people's weddings. If ever you wanted a step-by-step account of times past, they said to each other: ask Irene.

Irene rarely took herself through the evening before the day she was due to be married. But if she had to then she could have done it with no difficulty. It wasn't hard to remember the smells: the lilac in the garden, the polish on all the furniture, the orange blossom in the house. She even remembered the rich smell of the handcream that she was massaging carefully into her hands when she heard the door bell ring. It must be a late present, she thought, or possibly yet another fussy aunt who had come up from the country for the ceremony and arrived like a homing pigeon at the house.

She was surprised to hear Andrew's voice, talking to her younger sister downstairs. Andrew was meant to be at his home dealing with all his relations just as Irene had been doing. He had an uncle, a priest, flying in from the African Missions to assist at the wedding. Andrew's grandmother was a demanding old lady who regarded every gathering as in some way centring around her; Irene was surprised that Andrew had been allowed to escape.

Rosemary, her sister and one of the bridesmaids, had no interest in anything apart from the possible appearance of a huge spot on her face. She waved Andrew airily up the stairs.

'She's been up there titivating herself for hours,' Irene heard her say. Before she had time to react to Rosemary's tactlessness, Irene heard Andrew say 'Oh God,' in a funny, choked sort of voice, and before he even came into the room, she knew something was very wrong.

Andrew's face was as white as the dress that hung between sheets of tissue paper on the outside of the big mahogany wardrobe. His hands shook and trembled like the branches of the beautiful laburnum tree outside her window, the yellow blossom shaking in the summer breeze.

He tried to take her hand but she was covered in hand-cream. Irene decided that somehow it was imperative that she keep rubbing the cream still further in. It was like not walking on the crack in the road: if she kept massaging her hands then he couldn't take them in his, and he couldn't tell her what awful thing he was about to tell her.

On and on she went rhythmically, almost hypnotically, as if she were pulling on tight gloves. Her hands never stopped moving; her face never moved at all.

He fumbled for words, but Irene didn't help him.

The words came eventually, tumbling over each other, contradicting each other even, punctuated with apology and self-disgust. It wasn't that there was anyone else, Lord no, and it wasn't even as if he had stopped loving her, in many ways he had never loved her more than now, looking at her and knowing that he was destroying all their dreams and their hopes, but he had thought about it very seriously, and the truth was that he wasn't ready, he wasn't old enough, maybe technically he was old enough, but in his heart he didn't feel old enough to settle down, he wasn't certain enough that this was the Right Thing. For either of them, he added hastily, wanting Irene to know that it was in her interests as well as his.

On and on, she worked the cream into her hands and wrists; even a little way up her arms.

She sat impassively on her little blue bedroom-stool, her frilly dressing-table behind her. There were no tears, no tantrums. There were not even any words. Eventually he could speak no more.

'Oh Irene, say something for God's sake, tell me how much you hate me, what I've done to your life.' He almost begged to be railed against.

She spoke slowly, her voice was very calm. 'But of course I don't hate you,' she said, as if explaining something to a slow-witted child. 'I love you, I always will, and let's look at what you've done to my life ... You've changed it certainly ...' Her eyes fell on the wedding dress.

Andrew started again. Guilt and shame poured from him in a torrent released by her unexpected gentleness. He would take it upon himself to explain to everyone, he would tell her parents now. He would explain everything to the guests, he would see that the presents were returned. He would try to compensate her family financially for all the expense they had gone to. If everyone thought this was the right thing to do he would go abroad, to a faraway place like Australia or Canada or Africa ... somewhere they needed young lawyers, a place where nobody from here need ever look at him again and remember all the trouble he had caused.

And then suddenly he realized that he and he alone was doing the talking; Irene sat still, apart from those curious hand movements, as if she had not heard or understood what he was saying. A look of horror came over his face: perhaps she did not understand.

'I mean it, Irene,' he said simply. 'I really do mean it, you know, I wish I didn't.'

'I know you mean it.' Her voice was steady, her eyes were clear. She did understand.

Andrew clutched at a straw. 'Perhaps *you* feel the same. Perhaps we *both* want to get out of it? Is that what you are saying?' He was so eager to believe it, his face almost shone with enthusiasm.

But there was no quarter here. In a voice that didn't shake, with no hint of a tear in her eye, Irene said that she loved him and would always love him. But that it was far better, if he felt he couldn't go through with it, that this should be discovered the night before the marriage, rather than the night after. This way at least one of them would be free to make a different marriage when the time came.

'Well both of us, surely?' Andrew was bewildered.

Irene shook her head. 'I can't see myself marrying anyone else but you,' she said. There was no blame, regret, accusation. Just a statement.

In the big house, where three hundred guests were expected tomorrow, it was curiously silent. Perhaps the breeze had died down; they couldn't even hear the flapping of the edges of the marquee on the lawn.

The silence was too long between them. But Andrew knew she was not going to break it. 'So what will we do? First, I mean?' he asked her.

She looked at him pleasantly as if he had asked what record he should put on the player. She said nothing.

20

'Tell our parents, I suppose, yours first. Are they down-stairs?' he suggested.

'No, they're over at the golf club, they're having a little reception or drink or something for those who aren't coming tomorrow.'

'Oh God,' Andrew said.

There was another silence.

'Do you think we should go and tell *my* parents then? Grandmother will need some time to get adjusted . . .'

Irene considered this. 'Possibly,' she said. But it was unsatisfactory.

'Or maybe the caterers,' Andrew said. 'I saw them bustling around setting things up . . .' His voice broke. He seemed about to cry. 'Oh God, Irene, it's a terrible mess.'

'I know,' she agreed, as if they were talking about a rain cloud or some other unavoidable irritation to the day.

'And I suppose I should tell Martin, he's been fussing so much about the etiquette of it all and getting things in the right order. In a way he may be relieved . . .' Andrew gave a nervous little laugh but hastily corrected himself. 'But sorry, of course, mainly sorry, of course, very, very sorry that things haven't worked out.'

'Yes. Of course,' Irene agreed politely.

'And the bridesmaids? Don't you think we should tell Rosemary now, and Catherine? And that you should ring Rita and tell her . . . and tell her . . . that . . . well that . . .'

'Tell her what, exactly?'

'Well, tell her that we've changed our minds . . .'

'That you've changed your mind, to be strictly honest,' Irene said.

'Yes, but you agree,' he pleaded.

'What do I agree?'

'That if it is the Wrong Thing to do, then it were better we

21

know now than tomorrow when it's all too late and we are man and wife till death . . .' his voice ran out.

'Ah yes, but don't you see, I don't think we *are* doing the Wrong Thing getting married.'

'But you agreed . . .' He was in a panic.

'Oh, of course I agreed, Andrew, I mean what on earth would be the point of not agreeing? Naturally we can't go through with it. But that's not to say that *I'm* calling it off.'

'No, no, but does that matter as much as telling people . . . I mean now that we know that it won't take place, isn't it unfair to people to let them think that it will?'

'Yes and no.'

'But we can't have them making the food, getting dressed . . .'

'I know.' She was thoughtful.

'I want to do what's best, what's most fair,' Andrew said. And he did, Irene could see that, in the situation which he had brought about, he still wanted to be fair.

'Let's see,' she suggested. 'Who is going to be most hurt by all this?'

He thought about it. 'Your parents probably, they've gone to all this trouble . . .' He waved towards the garden where three hundred merrymakers had planned to stroll.

'No, I don't think they're the most hurt.'

'Well, maybe my uncle, the whole way back from Africa and he had to ask permission from a bishop. Or my grandmother . . . or the bridesmaids. They won't get a chance to dress up.' Andrew struggled to be fair.

'I think that I am the one who will be most hurt.' Irene's voice wasn't even slightly raised. It was as if she had given the problem equally dispassionate judgement.

'I mean, my parents have other daughters. There'll be Rosemary and Catherine, one day they'll have weddings. And your uncle, the priest . . . well he'll have a bit of a

22

holiday. No, I think I am the one who is *most* upset, I'm not going to marry the man I love, have the life I thought I was going to.'

'I know, I know.' He sounded like someone sympathizing over a bereavement.

'So I thought that perhaps you'd let me handle it *my* way.'

'Of course, Irene, that's why I'm here, whatever you say.'

'I say we shouldn't tell anyone anything. Not tonight.'

'I won't change my mind, in case that's what you're thinking.'

'Lord no, why should you? It's much too serious to be flitting about, chopping and changing.'

He handed their future into her hands. 'Do it whatever way you want. Just let me know and I'll do it.' He was prepared to pay any price to get the wedding called off.

But Irene didn't allow herself the time to think about that. 'Let me be the one not to turn up,' she said. 'Let me be seen to be the partner who had second thoughts. That way at least I get out of it with some dignity.'

He agreed. Grooms had been left standing at the altar before. He would always say afterwards that he had been greatly hurt but he respected Irene's decision.

'And you won't tell *anyone*?' she made him promise.

'Maybe Martin?' he suggested.

'Particularly not Martin, he'd give the game away. In the church you must be seen to be waiting for me.'

'But your father and mother . . . is it fair to leave it to the last minute?'

'They'd prefer to think that I let you down rather than the other way. Who wants a daughter who has been abandoned by the groom?'

'It's not that . . .' he began.

'I *know* that, silly, but not everyone else does.' She had stopped creaming her hands. They talked like old friends and conspirators. The thing would only succeed if nobody had an inkling.

'And afterwards . . .' He seemed very eager to know every step of her plan.

'Afterwards . . .' Irene was thoughtful. 'Oh, afterwards we can go along being friends . . . until you meet someone else . . . People will admire you, think you are very forgiving, too tolerant even . . . there'll be no awkwardness. No embarrassment.'

Andrew stood at the gate of the big house to wave goodbye; she sat by her window under the great laburnum tree and waved back. She was a girl in a million. What a pity he hadn't met her later. Or proposed to her later, when he was *ready* to be married. His stomach lurched at the thought of the mayhem they were about to unleash the following day. He went home with a heavy heart to hear stories of the Missions from his uncle the priest, and tales of long-gone grandeur from his grandmother.

Martin had read many books on being best man. Possibly too many.

'It's only natural for you to be nervous,' he said to Andrew at least forty times. 'It's only natural for you to worry about your speech, but remember the most important thing is to thank Irene's parents for giving her to you.'

When they heard the loud sniffs from Andrew's grandmother, the best man had soothing remarks also. 'It's only natural for elderly females to cry at weddings,' he said.

Andrew stood there, his stomach like lead. Since marriage was instituted, no groom had stood like this in the certain knowledge that his bride was not just a little late, or held up in traffic, or adjusting her veil – all the excuses that Martin was busy hissing into his ear.

He felt a shame like he had never known, allowing all these

three hundred people to assemble in a church for a ceremony that would not take place. He looked fearfully at the parish priest, and at his own uncle. It took some seconds for it to sink in that the congregation had risen to its feet, and that the organist had crashed into the familiar chords of 'Here Comes The Bride'.

He turned like any groom turns and saw Irene, perfectly at ease on her father's arm, smiling to the left and smiling to the right.

With his mouth wide open and his face whiter than the dress she wore, he looked into her eyes. He felt Martin's fingers in his ribs and he stepped forward to stand beside her.

Despite her famous recall, Irene never told that story to anyone. She only talked about it once to Andrew, on their honeymoon, when he tried to go over the events himself. And in all the years that followed, it had been *so* obvious that she had taken the right decision, run the right risk and realized that their marriage was the Right Thing, there was no point in talking about it at all.

Was Andrew also 'right', though? Does he sound ready for marriage? Have a look at all he says, his anxiety for himself, his tendency to project his own state of mind on to others, and his lack of consideration for Irene's feelings.

On the other hand, you may find evidence that he really loves her very much: where? Is it knowing this that makes Irene 'right'?

Such 'evidence', on which we build our discussion of these questions – the characters' actions, words, and tone – is the characterization.

In very few words the writer has also sketched a setting which is vivid but which supports the mood of the events: the smells of the house and the hand cream, the breeze in the laburnum and the marquee, and then the breeze falling still.

The viewpoint starts as Irene's (not knowing what Andrew's come to say) and shifts to his (not knowing how she is tricking him). But all this is within the much longer perspective of memory. The story seems kind and cheerful because it is told from Irene's thoughts many years later. Without that reassuring last paragraph we might have real doubts about the marriage.

Finally a point about the medium *being used. This story was written to be read aloud on BBC Radio. There the discussion between Andrew and Irene (most of the story) works particularly well by taking up 'real time' rather than being read rapidly by the eye.*

FOR FURTHER READING:

Any of Maeve Binchy's novels or stories: warm, frequently amusing fiction turning generally on family relationships.

GARRISON KEILLOR

★

Garrison Keillor writes about his home state of Minnesota, a
vast prairie region in the northern USA. In the mid-1970s he
started a radio show, where he regularly told stories bringing
news from the imaginary small town of Lake Wobegon. Here
every week is 'quiet' (the same first line begins each story),
and the narrator speaks in the present tense as a citizen of the
town, explaining its people to us as needed.

'Commencement' (first paragraph) is the high-school leav-
ers' ceremony (commencing the rest of their lives).

Dale

———————————— ★ ————————————

I

It has been a quiet week in Lake Wobegon. Commencement
was Wednesday evening at the football field, the eighty-seven
members of the Class of '86 were ushered into the next
chapter of their lives to the sweet strains of Elgar. Carla
Krebsbach was one of them, and earlier that day, while she
looked at the pictures of her classmates, autographed, in her
copy of *The Shore*, she thought, 'Wouldn't it be nice if there
were eighty-six people in the Class of '86? It would be like a
good omen,' and then it struck her that she had wished
someone dead, just as her eyes fell on Dale Uecker's picture,

where he had written, 'If you get to heaven before I do, just drill a hole and pull me through – Lots of love and good luck to a great kid, that's you!'

She thought, 'Dale is going to die because of my terrible thought.' With his black hair combed like he never combs it, serious eyes looking straight out, he looked like he might be dead already, hanging in his basement from a rafter, or drunk and crashed into a tree, or his head blown off. *Lord have mercy on me, a sinner*. She put on her eye shadow and prayed for God to save his life.

That night, at seven o'clock sharp, the eighty-seven moved in processional formation out of the gym door, across the dirt lot, and on to the cinder track around the field where the Leonards won two games last fall. To the sad and elegant cadence of 'Pomp and Circumstance', the Class passed before the bleachers and the sharp tiny flashes of light here and here and here like parents' heads exploding, and filed into the eight rows of folding chairs between the forty- and fifty-yard lines, and, on a signal from Miss Falconer, they sat down in unison. She had them practice in the lunchroom on Tuesday. She said, 'Don't flop down like that, don't just collapse like a pile of bricks – let yourself down gracefully – no, not like that! – you look like you're an invalid.'

She worked with them on the correct method of sitting and they got worse at it, until she threw up her hands in despair. She is a small, utterly elegant woman, so perfectly groomed and neatly dressed that if she dropped dead the undertaker wouldn't have to fix her up a bit – she's ready to go right straight in the coffin for review. So elegant, and she clapped her elegant hands and cried, 'What's the matter with you people? This is simple! Don't flop, don't poke around or grope or waggle your seats, just – *sit*. Dale? Dale, are you part of this, or what is your problem?'

Dale had reason to be distracted. He was fairly sure that

28

he'd flunked Dentley's final in higher algebra and that any
moment there'd be a knock on the door, Mr Halvorson
would come in and say, 'Dale, could I see you ... out here
... for a moment,' and his classmates would turn and look
and think, 'Heroin. Heroin and car theft and sex acts too
awful to mention.' He'd follow the principal out to the hall
and hear him say, 'I have bad news, Dale. You can't graduate,
you'll have to come back next year.' He waited all day for the
knock, he felt like he was floating. Tuesday afternoon they
got their copies of *The Shore* and sat on the grass where they
used to sit talking after lunch all those years and signed each
other's yearbooks. He wrote, 'Dear Allen, remember all the
good times we had – '

I will always remember this, he thought, this very moment;
years from now I'll always be able to remember exactly how
this looked and how I felt. I'll remember her face – looking at
Carla Krebsbach – and he looked where Carla had written in
his book:

> When darkest night surrounds you
> Look up and see a star
> And know that you have one true friend
> No matter where you are.

Algebra ordinarily was a good subject for him but on Monday
he couldn't remember anything the first twenty minutes. He
kept saying, 'Relax', and relaxed and got panicky in a relaxed
sort of way. The last thirty minutes he wrote down anything
he could think of that made sense. On the last problem, in the
last panicky minutes of the hour, he caught a clear view of
Barbara Soderberg's test – the problem solved in big block
lettering – and looked up at the top of Dentley's head behind
his desk, looked at Barbara's test again, and then looked up
at the minute hand just about to jump to the twelve so the

bells would ring, and thought, this doesn't matter that much, it's just not that important to me. And set his pencil down. The bell rang and Dale stood up and walked away. That was Monday.

There are no Ueckers in *Who's Who*, Dale has checked. He imagined how his name'd look in there and wrote it down on an index card that is pasted inside his blue folder where he keeps his school stuff.

UECKER, DALE. b. Lake Wobegon, Minn., March 4, 1968. BA Harvard, 1990. MA Yale, 1991. Ph.D. University of Paris, 1993. Married, Danielle Monteux, 1992. Three children: Antoine, Mimi, and Doug. Elected to the Institute of Arts, 1994, and L'Institut Nationale Académie de l'Honneur et Gloire et Héroisme, 1995. Author of numerous scholarly and artistic works, frequent lecturer here and abroad, recipient of more prizes than you could shake a stick at.

He thought of it again in the minute before the bell. He thought, Life is so wonderful that it is all we can do simply to experience it, and all the things people think are important – none of it matters if it makes us less able to live. Did I think of that myself? he wondered.

He wrote it on the front page of *The Shore* under a photograph of the school: I AM ALIVE. I AM A LIVING FEELING PERSON AND WHAT I USED TO THINK WAS SO IMPORTANT, IT ISN'T. TESTS AND GRADUATION DON'T MATTER BECAUSE NOW I KNOW WHAT I NEED TO KNOW, THAT THE IMPORTANT THING IS LIFE ITSELF.

How glorious to fail – and, in this moment of humiliation, discover the meaning of life.

It was the greatest day and a half of his life, and then it ended sadly. Dentley called him in and said, 'Dale, your final wasn't so good but I've been looking at it and I'm going to give you a C minus on it and a C for the year – I think that basically you understand the material, you just didn't know exactly how to use it.'

'But I didn't solve the problems,' Dale said.

'Yeah, but I could see where you were headed on most of them, and anyway I'm going to give you some extra credit for class participation.'

He looked up, a sad man with thin dry hair, smiling, and Dale said, 'That's not right. I flunked your test. I don't want to sneak out of it. I failed.'

'Dale, you had a bad day. I'm not going to nail you for that.'

He didn't feel right about it but he let Dentley write down a C, then he felt worse. It was like he had refused to cheat, only to allow someone else to cheat for him. He talked to Mr Halvorson, who thought Dale was complaining that the grade was low. He kept saying, 'Dale, there's no shame in getting a C—it's a passing grade.'

When he sat with the others Wednesday night, he felt good again. The night so clear, the smell of grass and damp, the music and voices drifting across the field, so many faces – how could a lover of life not be elated with so much to see as this? Carla won the Sons of Knute Shining Star scholarship and they all jumped up and clapped. She was valedictorian too. 'When we look back on this night years from now we will see it as a great moment when our lives turned and our future course was determined,' she said. At the end, the band played and they stood up together in a whoosh of gowns and walked out, heads high. Someone called, 'Dale! Dale!' and the camera flashed. He went with Allen to Martha Hedlund's, whose parents weren't home, and drank beer and smoked a cigarette. Carla said, 'Hi, Dale,' and he put his arm around her. They talked about what they would do in life. 'I'm going

31

in the Navy,' he said, which sounded good to him. A great night, drinking a can of beer, one arm around a girl, talking. And then she said, 'I'm awfully glad you're alive.'

'It's enough to be alive,' he said, 'a person doesn't need anything more.'

'The Navy!' said Allen. 'I thought we were going to go to Saint Cloud State together. How can you go in the Navy?'

'Just do it. That's how.'

Drinking a beer, one arm around a girl, talking about life – on the verge of leaving all this behind, on the very edge, the last moment before the door shuts, the last trembling moment – when she said that strange wonderful thing, 'I'm awfully glad you're alive.'

So was he, so glad he was awfully sorry to say good night.

2

Beautiful summer weather the week after graduation, a good week for fishing, when farmers got a lull in their field work and could go out and sit and rock in a boat and work on their sunburn. Rollie Hochstetter pulled in a stringerful of sunnies, fishing in Sunfish Bay, about twenty yards off the end of Kruegers' dock, not far from the weeds, with his brother-in-law Don Bauer in Don's aluminum boat (6½-horse-power motor), with 2½-to-3½-inch worms, about two feet off the bottom using a ¾-inch red plastic bobber. Nearby sat Clint Bunsen in his boat, contemplating the sun on the cool water, the rod and reel in his hand. His serenity was disturbed by the activity at Rollie's stringer, so he called over, 'You going to keep those puny things? I'm going for the big ones. I'm not sure those are legal-size, are they?'

Rollie said, 'You know, to tell you the truth, I don't go for those big ones, they're too damn bony. These medium-size are the good eaters, you know that.'

Clint contemplated the wisdom of Rollie: if you can't have something, find a reason why you wouldn't want it. He imagined Rollie as a monk in a boat, praying, 'Lord, do not send me any of those big ones as they are too bony, Lord, as Thou surely must know. Grant Thy servant a little fish, one of the good eaters.'

Clint knew why Rollie was out on the lake, though; it was because his heart was breaking. His grandson Dale Uecker decided to join the Navy, and who could say whether he'd come back or not?

'Why so soon?' his mother said. 'How do I know you've even *thought* about it? Four years! Dale! What's the big rush? You haven't signed anything yet, have you? Honey. You didn't. Oh, Dale. How could you do this? Honey, you don't even know how to swim. You'd be out in the ocean some-place.'

'Ma, they carry life preservers.'

'How do you know that?'

'It's the law. They have to.'

'Who's going to enforce it? This is the government, they make the law, they don't have to obey it, they don't hafta take care of you one bit – they could throw you over the side and who'd know it?'

Bobbie was scared and upset. Dale is her youngest boy, then it's Deb, and then they're all gone. She stood against the stove, crying into a dish towel. (This was a week ago Friday.) Everyone was there, an emergency family meeting, Rollie and Louise and Jack and Bobbie and Dale's uncle Carl. Bobbie said, '*Talk to him, Jack.*' 'I can't tell him anything, I gave up telling him anything a long time ago,' said Jack. Bobbie said, 'Talk to him, Dad,' and Rollie just looked away. He was hurt because Dale hadn't asked his advice.

Bobbie was making lasagne. 'What am I doing this for?' she said through her tears. It was eight o'clock in the evening and everyone had eaten supper and she was making four big pans of lasagne, to freeze, she said, but with Dale leaving and taking his appetite with him, why such big pans?

'This is the craziest thing you ever did and you did some crazy ones,' she said. She laughed. 'Remember when you went after the groundhogs?' He certainly did. It was only a year ago. Something was harvesting their garden as the plants came up out of the ground, and one day Jack noticed six groundhogs hiking through the yard en route to the lunch programme and thought, Six is too many. One or two, yes (if they're married), but six is pushing charity too far, so he told Dale, 'Dale, get out there and wipe out those groundhogs.'

Dale got his .22 out of his closet and was coming downstairs when he caught sight of himself in the mirror. He wasn't wearing a shirt, and standing there, nice tan, fairly good pectoral development, rifle, he looked like a hero. He found a red bandanna and tied it around his forehead. Looked better.

Outside, leaning against the tree behind the corncrib, waiting for groundhogs in the scorching heat, he could imagine how good he looked, and he moved out through the weeds, imagining other men – Bravo Company – following him (though he couldn't hear them, that's how good they were). He nailed the first groundhog by the milkhouse. It flopped twice and he heard others scurry into the weeds at the end of the garden. One of them made a run for it. He fired and missed, and chased it, and then saw one at eight o'clock and turned and crouched and fired, but it was a big rock, not a groundhog, and the bullet hit it and then he heard a *chunk* and there was a hole in the side of their green Chevy.

She laughed at the thought of it, her boy at supper that night saying, 'Dad, I was going after groundhogs today and I put a shell in the Chevy.' The reason Dale waited until supper to confess was that his mom was weeding begonias on the other side of the car. He stood on the rock and looked at the hole and saw that if the car hadn't been parked there he would've killed her. He put the rifle back in his room.

She laughed, 'Oh honey, I'm sorry, but it was so comical, the look on your face –' He might have killed her that afternoon and been in all the newspapers as a wacko teenager.

She said, 'But what are you going to do with the nice car Grandpa gave you?'

'Well,' he said, 'it'll be just as nice in four years, except it won't have so much mileage on it.'

Rollie didn't say much that night, because he felt too bad. He had looked after Dale since he was six – Rollie saw how those older brothers ganged up on the little boy and he knew what a hard man Jack could be, so he went out of his way for Dale and tried to show him things. He taught him how to drive a tractor when he was seven, and how to handle pigs, and took him fishing, and was close to him, as close as Rollie knew how to be, close enough that Dale came over to talk to his grandpa every single damn day, so he was hurt that the boy would now turn away and be secretive and, this Friday night, not even look at him. Rollie sat and studied his coffee. 'You know,' he said, 'there never was a war we fought that we had a good reason for. None of them made sense. Not a goddamned one.'

Jack cleared his throat. Everyone was quiet. Nobody spoke.

About eleven, Bobbie said she was going to bed. They walked out in the yard and stood around the cars for a while, talking. To Dale it was like a dream. Under the yard light and the stars in the sky, his family talking in the evening breeze, the big barn half full of hay bales like a cargo ship docked at the house, looming above them in the night.

35

Saturday he and his dad went out and cut more hay, and Sunday more relatives came over. He tried to call Carla but she was at her grandparents' fiftieth anniversary in Cold Spring, and in the evening she was gone, her mother said, to Saint Cloud with friends to see a movie. What friends? What was his name? Dale didn't dare ask, but he did drive past her house about eleven o'clock. The lights were on, but he didn't dare go in. He was afraid that if he said, 'I came to say goodbye, I'm going into the Navy, who knows if I'll ever come back,' she'd say, 'Oh, that's interesting. Well, good luck.'

Monday he cleaned out his room. He threw out all his school stuff, most of his letters, and his 4-H project on pork (Nature's Perfect Food), and selected the pictures he'd take along, including Carla's graduation picture, an enlargement. Most other people she gave a billfold-size but to him she gave an enlargement, one more way he knew she had feelings for him.

He called the Navy the next day and went to Saint Cloud and took all the tests and made up his mind that if they wanted him he was going.

'You seem almost happy about it or something,' Allen said. 'It's like you don't even care or anything.'

The reason he felt happy was the Navy physical. As the doctor sat and asked him questions, Dale was making up his mind to ask him one, and finally, after he lowered his underpants and coughed and was checked for a hernia, Dale said, 'I, uh, was always wondering why, uh, my pennis, you know, it hangs crooked. I always wondered what was wrong with it.' The doctor looked. He said, 'First of all, it's pronounced "penis", and secondly, it's perfectly normal.'

Perfectly normal. What a gift. He took it home with him. *Perfectly normal.* He had worried about this since he was sixteen. He wanted to call Carla and tell her somehow, or at least be with her and feel perfectly normal. He was glad he had never discussed it with her and mispronounced 'penis'. Somehow the subject had never come up.

And suddenly it was Wednesday noon and Dale was leaving at one. His mother sat and wept over breakfast and then she got busy. Jack drove the Pontiac in to fill it up with gas, a sort of going-away present, a full tank. Dale sat in the living room. Debbie sat there, reading *Parents* magazine. Everyone came in for a little lunch, the Ueckers and Rollie and Louise and Carl. They squeezed in around the kitchen table, where his mother had laid out a big spread. She didn't use the dining room, because it wasn't Sunday and they weren't company. And she felt too bad. She felt so bad she had spent all morning fixing lunch. There were platters of meat, hot and cold, and tuna salad and potato salad and hamburger hotdish and tuna hotdish and breads and pickles – even Fran could see it was too much – and then she reached into the oven for the big one, a baking pan. She held it out to him – 'For you, Dale' – and she took the tinfoil off. It was pigs in blankets, wieners baked into a biscuit crust. He had liked them when he was eight but she still thought it was his favourite dish. She watched him take two. She studied his face for signs of pleasure. 'Mmmmmmm, those are very very good. Thank you,' he said.

And then it was one. 'Well,' he said. He stood up. 'I can't stand it,' she cried, and she ran into the bathroom. He hugged his grandpa and grandma, he shook hands with Uncle Carl, he looked at his dad and shook hands with him. He said, 'Ma? Come on, Ma.' And then he set down his duffel bag. 'Did you give me back the car keys?' he said to his dad. Jack said, 'I gave em to you, of course I did, you musta put em in the kitchen.'

But they weren't anywhere in the kitchen. Everyone helped look except his mom, who was crying in the bathroom about

37

her boy leaving. Except he wasn't leaving. 'Look in your pants,' Jack said. 'Dad, I didn't *put* em in my pants. You had em.'

'I gave em to you, Dale. I come home and got outta the car and come in and *give* em to ya. Look upstairs, look in the living room. Where were ya sitting? Try and think.'

Grandma was crying now, and Debbie had an arm around her and was sniffling. Oh Dale, we may never see him again. Dale thought: *I may never get out of here.* His dad standing by the fridge saying: 'This is stupid. This is the craziest thing I ever heard of.' Carl: 'Just calm down, Jack.' Jack: 'What are you talking about? I'm calm.' Rollie: 'Take it easy.' Jack: 'Why don't *you* take it easy, Dad?'

'Ma, come on out of there. Open the door.'

'I can't. I feel too bad.'

'Ma, are my car keys in there?'

'No.'

'Ma, are you sure?'

'No.'

'Ma, please. I got to go. Help me find them.'

'But I don't want you to go.'

'Ma, did you take my keys?'

'No.'

'Ma!'

His grandma crying. 'I just know I'll never see you again.'

Debbie crying. 'I'll be here, Grandma.'

'Oh I know, honey, but it's not the same.'

Debbie went up to her room to cry.

Jack said, 'Maybe you gave em to someone. Maybe you left em out on the lawn somewhere. Maybe you left em in the *car*.' When he said that, a thoughtful look came over his face. 'You know,' he said, 'I wonder if they wouldn't be up over the visor.'

And of course they were.

And so he left.

He drove past Carla's on the odd chance she'd be outside, and she was mowing the lawn and he got out to say goodbye and she hugged him. 'I'll sure miss you a lot,' she said, 'so I hope you'll write me once in a while.'

And away he went. It's a wonderful thing to push on alone toward the horizon and have it be your own horizon and not someone else's. It's a good feeling, lonely and magnificent and frightening and peaceful, especially when you leave someone behind who will miss you and to whom you can write.

And so the blue Pontiac rose over the rise and zoomed around the curve by the grain elevator and up the long grade to the hill and disappeared into the future.

The plot is 'quiet', everyday, and open (no secrets held back from us); but it's still a big story for Dale and his family. The collection from which it comes is called Leaving Home, *which we nearly all do at some point in our growing-up, particularly in rural areas; and which is a major step.*

To interest us, a plot doesn't have to be about exceptional occurrences. Garrison Keillor's material is the humour and pain and warmth in ordinary life; and there are potential stories like this in us all. The comic details are around us; the challenge is to notice them and get them down on paper. For example: Carla discovering that she has, in a sense, wished Dale dead; Dale's anxiety about being called out of class; his imaginary Who's Who *entry; and his disappointment at discovering he has been passed, when he has spent 'the greatest day and a half of his life' persuading himself how glorious it is to fail. (A bit like Rollie with the fish?) Or the tendency of a mother to assume that the dish you liked most at the age of eight is still your favourite; and her spending 'all morning fixing lunch' as a*

39

way of dealing with her grief. These, of course, are all brilliant touches of characterization; and you can find many more.

Keillor's casual colloquial style doesn't appear to strain for comic effect – even the idea that Miss Falconer will need no fixing by the undertaker sounds earnestly reasonable. Watch out particularly for him when he is straight-faced: 'She put on her eye shadow and prayed to God . . . ' (p. 28); 'like parents' heads exploding' (p. 28), or 'Somehow the subject had never come up.' (p. 37).

One way to study Keillor's skills is to try to match him, in a story from your own life – amusing, by all means, but realistic rather than exaggerated. The more realistic the more amusing, probably.

FOR FURTHER READING:

Lake Wobegon Days and *Leaving Home* by Garrison Keillor (Faber). Also, almost anything by Mark Twain, in some respects Keillor's ancestor; the best of all is *Huckleberry Finn* (many editions).

J. G. BALLARD

★

J. G. Ballard was born in 1930 in Shanghai, China, where his
father was a businessman, and with his family was imprisoned
by the Japanese during the Second World War. He describes
this experience in his novel *Empire of the Sun*, and it also
influences the science fiction for which he is best known.

Ballard specializes in visions of disaster, decay after technological excess, or future desolation. Like many SF writers, he
often seems to be warning contemporary society: 'This is
what will happen if we go on this way'. When this story was
first published, 1985 was still in the future.

Having a Wonderful Time

──────────── ★ ────────────

3 JULY 1985
Hotel Imperial, Playa Inglaterra, Las Palmas

We arrived an hour ago after an amazing flight. For some
reason of its own the Gatwick computer assigned us to first
class seats, along with a startled dentist from Bristol, her
husband and three children. Richard, as ever fearful of flying,
took full advantage of the free champagne and was five miles
high before the wheels left the ground. I've marked our
balcony on the twenty-seventh floor. It's an extraordinary
place, about twenty miles down the coast from Las Palmas, a

41

brand new resort complex with every entertainment conceivable, all arranged by bedside push-button. I'm just about to dial an hour's water-skiing, followed by Swedish massage and the hairdresser! *Diana*.

10 JULY
Hotel Imperial

An unbelievable week! I've never crammed so much excitement into a few days – tennis, scuba-diving, water-skiing, rounds of cocktail parties. Every evening a group of us heads for the boîtes and cabarets along the beach, ending up at one or more of the five nightclubs in the hotel. I've hardly seen Richard. The handsome cavalier in the picture is the so-called Beach Counsellor, a highly intelligent ex-public relations man who threw it all in two years ago and has been here ever since. This afternoon he's teaching me to hang-glide. Wish me happy landings! *Diana*.

17 JULY
Hotel Imperial

The times of sand are running out. Sitting here on the balcony, watching Richard ski-chute across the bay, it's hard to believe we'll be in Exeter tomorrow. Richard swears the first thing he'll do is book next year's holiday. It really has been an amazing success – heaven knows how they do it at the price, there's talk of a Spanish government subsidy. In part it's the unobtrusive but highly sophisticated organization – not a hint of Butlins, though it's British-run and we're all, curiously, from the West Country. Do you realize that Richard and I have been so busy we haven't once bothered to visit

Las Palmas? (Late news-flash: Mark Hastings, the Beach Counsellor, has just sent orchids to the room!) I'll tell you all about him tomorrow. *Diana.*

18 JULY
Hotel Imperial

Surprise! That computer again. Apparently there's been some muddle at the Gatwick end, our aircraft won't be here until tomorrow at the earliest. Richard is rather worried about not getting to the office today. We blew the last of our traveller's cheques, but luckily the hotel have been marvellous, thanks largely to Mark. Not only will there be no surcharge, but the desk clerk said they would happily advance us any cash we need. Hey-ho ... A slight let-down, all the same. We walked along the beach this afternoon, together for the first time. I hadn't realized how vast this resort complex actually is – it stretches for miles along the coast and half of it's still being built. Everywhere people were coming in on the airport buses from Sheffield and Manchester and Birmingham, within half an hour they're swimming and water-skiing, lounging around the hundreds of pools with their duty-free Camparis. Seeing them from the outside, as it were, it's all rather strange. *Diana.*

25 JULY
Hotel Imperial

Still here. The sky's full of aircraft flying in from Gatwick and Heathrow, but none of them, apparently, is ours. Each morning we've waited in the lobby with our suitcases packed, but the airport bus never arrives. After an hour or so the

desk clerk rings through that there's been a postponement
and we trudge back to another day by the pool, drinks and
water-skiing on the house. For the first few days it was rather
amusing, though Richard was angry and depressed. The
company is a major Leyland supplier, and if the axe falls,
middle-management is the first to feel it. But the hotel have
given us unrestricted credit, and Mark says that as long as we
don't go over the top they'll probably never bother to collect.
Good news: the company have just cabled Richard telling
him not to worry. Apparently hordes of people have been
caught the same way. An immense relief – I wanted to phone
you, but for days now all the lines have been blocked. *Diana*.

15 AUGUST
Hotel Imperial

Three more weeks! Hysterical laughter in paradise ... the
English papers flown in here are full of it, no doubt you've
heard that there's going to be a government inquiry. Apparently, instead of flying people back from the Canaries the
airlines have been sending their planes on to the Caribbean to
pick up the American holiday traffic. So the poor British are
stuck here indefinitely. There are literally hundreds of us in
the same boat. The amazing thing is that one gets used to it.
The hotel people are charm itself, they've pulled out all the
stops, organizing extra entertainments of every kind. There's a
very political cabaret, and an underwater archaeology team is
going to raise a Spanish caravel from the sea floor. To fill in the
time I'm joining an amateur theatrical group, we're thinking of
putting on *The Importance of Being Earnest*. Richard takes it all
with surprising calm. I wanted to post this from Las Palmas,
but there are no buses running, and when we set out on foot
Richard and I lost ourselves in a maze of building sites. *Diana*.

5 SEPTEMBER
Hotel Imperial

No news yet. Time moves like a dream. Every morning a crowd of bewildered people jam the lobby, trying to find news of their flights back. On the whole, everyone's taking it surprisingly well, showing that true British spirit. Most of them, like Richard, are management people in industry, but the firms, thank heavens, have been absolutely marvellous and cabled us all to get back when we can. Richard comments cynically that with present levels of industrial stagnation, and with the Government footing the bill, they're probably glad to see us here. Frankly, I'm too busy with a hundred and one activities to worry – there's a sort of mini-Renaissance of the arts going on. Mixed saunas, cordon bleu classes, encounter groups, the theatre, of course, and marine biology. Incidentally, we never did manage to get into Las Palmas. Richard hired a pedalo yesterday and set off up the coast. Apparently the entire island is being divided into a series of huge self-contained holiday complexes – human reserves, Richard called them. He estimates that there are a million people here already, mostly English working class from the north and midlands. Some of them have apparently been here for a year, living quite happily, though their facilities are nowhere as good as ours. Dress rehearsal tonight. Think of me as Lady Bracknell – it's mortifying that there's no one else quite mature enough to play the part, they're all in their twenties and thirties, but Tony Johnson, the director, an ex-ICI stat-istician, is being awfully sweet about it. *Diana.*

6 OCTOBER
Hotel Imperial

Just a brief card. There was a crisis this morning when Richard, who's been very moody recently, finally came into collision with the hotel management. When I went into the lobby after my French conversation class a huge crowd had gathered, listening to him rant away at the desk clerks. He was very excited but extremely logical in a mad way, demanding a taxi (there are none here, no one ever goes anywhere) to take him into Las Palmas. Baulked, he insisted on being allowed to phone the Governor of the Islands, or the Swiss Consul. Mark and Tony Johnson then arrived with a doctor. There was a nasty struggle for a moment, and then they took him up to our room. I thought he was completely out, but half an hour later, when I left the shower, he'd vanished. I hope he's cooling off somewhere. The hotel management have been awfully good, but it did surprise me that no one tried to intervene. They just watched everything in a glazed way and wandered back to the pool. Sometimes I think they're in no hurry to get home. *Diana.*

12 NOVEMBER
Hotel Imperial

An extraordinary thing happened today – I saw Richard for the first time since he left. I was out on the beach for my morning jog when there he was, sitting by himself under an umbrella. He looked very tanned and healthy, but much slimmer. He calmly told me a preposterous story about the entire Canaries being developed by the governments of Western Europe, in collusion with the Spanish authorities, as a kind of permanent holiday camp for their unemployables, not just the factory workers but most of the management people too. According to Richard there is a beach being built for the French on the other side of the island, and another for the Germans. And the Canaries are only one of many sites around the Mediterranean and Caribbean. Once there, the holiday-makers will never be allowed to return home, for fear of starting revolutions. I tried to argue with him, but he casually stood up and said he was going to form a resistance group, then strode away along the beach. The trouble is that he's found nothing with which to occupy his mind – I wish he'd join our theatre group, we're now rehearsing Pinter's *The Birthday Party*. *Diana*.

10 JANUARY 1986
Hotel Imperial

A sad day. I meant to send you a cable, but there's been too much to do. Richard was buried this morning, in the new international cemetery in the hills overlooking the bay. I've marked his place with an X. I'd last seen him two months ago, but I gather he'd been moving around the island, living in the half-constructed hotels and trying unsuccessfully to set up his resistance group. A few days ago he apparently stole an unseaworthy motor-boat and set off for the African coast. His body was washed ashore yesterday on one of the French beaches. Sadly, we'd completely lost touch, though I feel the experience has given me a degree of insight and maturity which I can put to good use when I play Clytemnestra in Tony's new production of *Electra*. He and Mark Hastings have been pillars of strength. *Diana*.

J. G. BALLARD

3 JULY 1986
Hotel Imperial

Have I really been here a year? I'm so out of touch with
England that I can hardly remember when I last sent a
postcard to you. It's been a year of the most wonderful
theatre, of parts I would once never have dreamed of playing,
and of audiences so loyal that I can hardly bear the thought
of leaving them. The hotels are full now, and we play to a
packed house every night. There's so much to do here, and
everyone is so fulfilled, that I rarely find the time to think of
Richard. I very much wish you were here, with Charles
and the children – but you probably are, at one of the
thousand hotels along the beach. The mails are so erratic, I
sometimes think that all my cards to you have never been
delivered, but lie unsorted with a million others in the vaults
of the shabby post office behind the hotel. Love to all of you.
Diana.

*Ballard's fiction is full of derelict aircraft, hotels, and cities:
twentieth-century 'progress' on the scrap-heap. Here it may
seem at first that we are in a very different picture – an endless
happy holiday, teeming beaches, new resorts being built. But
what lies behind it are 'the present levels of industrial stagnation'
and millions of people who are 'unemployables'; and that final
image of millions of postcards unsorted reveals that Playa
Inglaterra has become a vast human junkyard. It's a warning
all right.*

*This is the ultimate one-sided correspondence, since we suspect
at the end that nobody has ever seen it. All we are given is
postcards, and only from one person. What is the effect of*

deciding to tell the story this way? (This is three questions, really: about viewpoint, about style, and about characterization.)

FOR FURTHER READING:

For science fiction enthusiasts, almost anything by J. G. Ballard; alternatively, for an exceptional autobiographical story, read *Empire of the Sun*. The publisher is Cape. Also: *Brave New World* by Aldous Huxley (Penguin) – the classic novel which foresaw as long ago as 1932 a technological society which controls its mass population by providing them with an endless 'wonderful time'.

ELIZABETH BOWEN

Elizabeth Bowen (1899–1973) was born in Dublin, but lived most of her life in England, a widely admired novelist and short story writer.

'Maria' is set some time after the First World War, in a middle-class English society which no longer exists; see it as a costume drama. Here 'Indian children' means those of British people working in India, and the worrying 'tendencies' of the curate, Mr Hammond, are 'High Church' leanings towards Roman Catholicism.

Maria

'We have girls of our own, you see,' Mrs Dosely said, smiling warmly.

That seemed to settle it. Maria's aunt, Lady Rimlade, relaxed at last in Mrs Dosely's armchair, and, glancing round once more at the Rectory drawing room's fluttery white curtains, alert-looking photographs, and silver cornets spuming out pink sweet pea, consigned Maria to these pleasant influences.

'Then that will be delightful,' she said in that blandly conclusive tone in which she declared open so many bazaars. 'Thursday *next*, then, Mrs Dosely, about tea-time?'

'That will be delightful.'

'It is *most* kind,' Lady Rimlade concluded.

50

Maria could not agree with them. She sat scowling under her hat-brim, tying her gloves into knots. Evidently, she thought, I *am* being paid for.

Maria thought a good deal about money; she had no patience with other people's affectations about it, for she enjoyed being a rich little girl. She was only sorry not to know how much they considered her worth; having been sent out to walk in the garden while her aunt had just a short chat, dear, with the Rector's wife. The first phase of the chat, about her own character, she had been able to follow perfectly as she wound her way in and out of some crescent-shaped lobelia beds under the drawing room window. But just as the two voices changed – one going unconcerned, one very, very diffident – Mrs Dosely approached the window and, with an air of immense unconsciousness, shut it. Maria was balked.

Maria was at one of those comfortable schools where everything is attended to. She was (as she had just heard her Aunt Ena explaining to Mrs Dosely) a motherless girl, sensitive, sometimes difficult, deeply reserved. At school they took all this, with her slight tendency to curvature and her dislike of all puddings, into loving consideration. She was having her character 'done' for her – later on, when she came out, would be time for her hair and complexion. In addition to this, she learnt swimming, dancing, some French, the more innocent aspects of history, and *noblesse oblige*. It was a really nice school. All the same, when Maria came home for the holidays they could not do enough to console her for being a motherless girl who had been sent away.

Then, late last summer term, with inconceivable selfishness, her Uncle Philip fell ill and, in fact, nearly died. Aunt Ena had written less often and very distractedly, and when Maria came home she was told, with complete disregard for her motherlessness, that her uncle and aunt would be starting at once for a cruise, and that she was 'to be arranged for.'

ELIZABETH BOWEN

This was not so easy. All the relations and all the family
friends (who declared when Sir Philip was ill they'd do
anything in the world), wrote back their deep disappointment
at being unable to have Maria just now, though there was
nothing, had things been otherwise, that they would have
enjoyed more. One to his farm in fact, said Mr MacRobert,
the vicar, when he was consulted, another to his merchandise.
Then he suggested his neighbours, a Mr and Mrs Dosely, of
Malton Peele. He came over to preach in Lent; Lady Rimlade
had met him; he seemed such a nice man, frank, cheerful and
earnest. *She* was exceedingly motherly, everyone said, and
sometimes took in Indian children to make ends meet. The
Doselys would be suitable, Maria's aunt felt at once. When
Maria raged, she drew down urbane pink eyelids and said she
did wish Maria would not be rude. So she drove Maria and
the two little griffons over the next afternoon to call upon
Mrs Dosely. If Mrs Dosely really seemed sympathetic, she
thought she might leave the two little dogs with her too.

'And Mrs Dosely has girls of her own, she tells me,' said
Lady Rimlade on the way home. 'I should not wonder if you
made quite friends with them. I should not wonder if it was
they who had done the flowers. I thought the flowers were
done very nicely; I noticed them. Of course, I do not care
myself for small silver vases like that, shaped like cornets, but
I thought the effect in the Rectory drawing room very cheerful
and homelike.'

Maria took up the word skilfully. 'I suppose no one,' she
said, 'who has not been in my position can be expected to
realize what it feels like to have no home.'

'Oh, Maria darling . . . '

'I can't tell you what I think of this place you're sending
me to,' said Maria. 'I bounced on the bed in that attic they're
giving me and it's like iron. I suppose you realize that rectories
are always full of diseases? Of course, I shall make the best of

52

it, Aunt Ena. I shouldn't like you to feel I'd complained. But of course you don't realize a bit, do you, what I may be exposed to? So often carelessness about a girl at my age just ruins her life.'

Aunt Ena said nothing; she settled herself a little further down in the rugs and lowered her eyelids as though a strong wind were blowing.

That evening, on her way down to shut up the chickens, Mrs Dosely came upon Mr Hammond, the curate, rolling the cricket pitch in the Rectory field. He was indefatigable, and, though more High Church than they cared for, had outdoor tastes. He came in to meals with them regularly, 'as an arrangement', because his present landlady could not cook and a young man needs to be built up, and her girls were still so young that no one could possibly call Mrs Dosely designing. So she felt she ought to tell him.

'We shall be one more now in the house,' she said, 'till the end of the holidays. Lady Rimlade's little niece Maria – about fifteen – is coming to us while her uncle and aunt are away.'

'Jolly,' said Mr Hammond sombrely, hating girls.

'We *shall* be a party, shan't we?'

'The more the merrier, I dare say,' said Mr Hammond. He was a tall young man with a jaw, rather saturnine; he never said much, but Mrs Dosely expected family life was good for him. 'Let 'em all come,' said Mr Hammond, and went on rolling. Mrs Dosely, with a tin bowl under one arm and a basket hooked on the other, stood at the edge of the pitch and watched him.

'She seemed a dear little thing – not pretty, but such a serious little face, full of character. An only child, you see. I said to her when they were going away that I expected she and Dilly and Doris would soon be inseparable, and her face quite lit up. She has no mother; it seems so sad.'

53

'*I* never had a mother,' said Mr Hammond, tugging the roller grimly.

'Oh, I do *know*. But for a young girl I do think it still sadder ... I thought Lady Rimlade charming; so unaffected. I said to her that we all lived quite simply here, and that if Maria came we should treat her as one of ourselves, and she said that was just what Maria would love ... In age, you see, Maria comes just between Dilly and Doris.'

She broke off; she couldn't help thinking how three years hence Maria might well be having a coming-out dance. Then she imagined herself telling her friend Mrs Brotherhood: 'It's terrible, I never seem to see anything of my girls nowadays. They seem always to be over at Lady Rimlade's.'

'We must make the poor child feel at home here,' she told Mr Hammond brightly.

The Doselys were accustomed to making the best of Anglo-Indian children, so they continued to be optimistic about Maria. 'One must make allowance for character', had become the watchword of this warm-hearted household, through which passed a constant stream of curates with tendencies, servants with tempers, unrealized lady visitors, and yellow-faced children with no morale. Maria was forbearingly swamped by the family; she felt as though she were trying to box an eiderdown. Doris and Dilly had indelibly creased cheeks: they kept on smiling and smiling. Maria couldn't decide how best to be rude to them; they taxed her resourcefulness. She could not know Dilly had thought, 'Her face is like a sick monkey's', or that Doris, who went to one of those sensible schools, decided as soon that a girl in a diamond bracelet was shocking bad form. Dilly had repented at once of her unkind thought (though she had not resisted noting it in her diary), and Doris had simply said: 'What a pretty bangle. Aren't you afraid of losing it?' Mr Dosely thought Maria striking-looking (she had a pale, square-jawed little face, with a straight fringe cut above scowling brows), striking but disagreeable – here he gave a kind of cough in his thoughts and, leaning forward, asked Maria if she were a Girl Guide.

Maria said she hated the sight of Girl Guides, and Mr Dosely laughed heartily and said that this was a pity, because, if so, she must hate the sight of Doris and Dilly. The supper table rocked with merriment. Shivering in her red *crêpe* frock (it was a rainy August evening, the room was fireless, a window stood open, and outside the trees streamed coldly), Maria looked across at the unmoved Mr Hammond, square-faced, set and concentrated over his helping of macaroni cheese. He was not amused. Maria had always thought curates giggled; she despised curates because they giggled, but was furious with Mr Hammond for not giggling at all. She studied him for some time, and, as he did not look up, at last said: 'Are you a Jesuit?'

Mr Hammond (who had been thinking about the cricket pitch) started violently; his ears went crimson; he sucked in one last streamer of macaroni. 'No,' he said, 'I am not a Jesuit. Why?'

'Oh, nothing,' said Maria. 'I just wondered. As a matter of fact, I don't know what Jesuits are.'

Nobody felt quite comfortable. It was a most unfortunate thing, in view of the nature of Mr Hammond's tendencies, for poor little Maria, in innocence, to have said. Mr Hammond's tendencies were so marked, and, knowing how marked the Doselys thought his tendencies were, he was touchy. Mrs Dosely said she expected Maria must be very fond of dogs. Maria replied that she did not care for any dogs but alsatians. Mrs Dosely was glad to be able to ask Mr Hammond if it were not he who had told her that he had a cousin who bred alsatians. Mr Hammond said that this was the case. 'But unfortunately,' he added, looking across at Maria, 'I dislike alsatians intensely.'

Maria now realized with gratification that she had incurred the hatred of Mr Hammond. This was not bad for one evening. She swished her plateful of macaroni round with her fork then put the fork down pointedly. Undisguised wholesomeness was, in food as in personalities, repellent to Maria. 'This is the last supper but three – no, but two,' she said to herself, 'that I shall eat at this Rectory.'

It had all seemed so simple, it seemed so simple still, yet five nights afterwards found her going to bed once again in what Mrs Dosely called the little white nest that we keep for our girl friends. Really, if one came to look at it one way, the Doselys were an experience for Maria, who had never till now found anybody who could stand her when she didn't mean to be stood. French maids, governesses, highly paid, almost bribed into service, had melted away. There was something marvellously, memorably un-winning about Maria ... Yet here she still was. She had written twice to her aunt that she couldn't sleep and couldn't eat here, and feared she must be unwell, and Lady Rimlade wrote back advising her to have a little talk about all this with Mrs Dosely. Mrs Dosely, Lady Rimlade pointed out, was motherly. Maria told Mrs Dosely she was afraid she was unhappy and couldn't be well. Mrs Dosely exclaimed at the pity this was, but at all costs – Maria would see? – Lady Rimlade must not be worried. She had so expressly asked not to be worried at all.

'And she's so *kind*,' said Mrs Dosely, patting Maria's hand.

Maria simply thought, This woman is mad. She said with a wan smile that she was sorry, but having her hand patted gave her pins and needles. But rudeness to Mrs Dosely was like dropping a pat of butter on to a hot plate – it slid and melted away.

In fact, all this last week Maria's sole consolation had been Mr Hammond. Her pleasure in Mr Hammond was so intense that three days after her coming he told Mrs Dosely he didn't think he'd come in for meals any more, thank you, as his landlady had by now learned to cook. Even so, Maria had managed to see quite a lot of him. She rode round the village after him, about ten yards behind, on Doris's bicycle; she was there when he offered a prayer with the Mothers' Union; she never forgot to come out when he was at work on the cricket pitch ('Don't you seem to get rather hot,' she would ask him feelingly, as he mopped inside his collar. 'Or are you really not as hot as you seem?'), and, having discovered that at six every evening he tugged a bell, then read Evensong in the church to two ladies, she came in alone every evening and sat in the front pew, looking up at him. She led the responses, waiting courteously for Mr Hammond when he lost his place.

But tonight Maria came briskly, mysteriously up to the little white nest, locking the door for fear Mrs Dosely might come in to kiss her good night. She could now agree that music was inspiring. For they had taken her to the Choral Society's gala, and the effect it had had on Maria's ideas was stupendous. Half way through a rondo called 'Off to the Hills' it had occurred to her that when she got clear of the Rectory she would go off to Switzerland, stay in a Palace Hotel, and do a little climbing. She would take, she thought, a hospital nurse, in case she hurt herself climbing, and an alsatian to bother the visitors in the hotel. She had glowed – but towards the end of 'Hey, nonny, nonny' a finer and far more constructive idea came along, eclipsing the other. She clapped her handkerchief to her mouth and, conveying to watchful Dilly that she might easily be sick at any moment, quitted the schoolhouse hurriedly. Safe in her white nest, she put her candlestick down with a bump, got her notepaper out, and sweeping her hairbrushes off the dressing table, sat down at it to write thus:

Dearest Aunt Ena: You must wonder why I have not

written for so long. The fact is, all else has been swept from my mind by one great experience. I hardly know how to put it all into words. The fact is I love a Mr Hammond, who is the curate here, and am loved by him, we are engaged really and hope to be married quite shortly. He is a fascinating man, extremely High Church, he has no money but I am quite content to live with him as a poor man's wife as I shall have to do if you and Uncle Philip are angry, though you may be sorry when I bring my little children to your door to see you. If you do not give your consent we shall elope but I am sure, dear Aunt Ena, that you will sympathize with your little niece in her great happiness. All I beseech is that you will not take me away from the Rectory; I do not think I could live without seeing Wilfred every day – or every night rather, as we meet in the churchyard and sit on a grave with our arms round each other in the moonlight. The Doselys do not know as I felt it was my duty to tell you first, but I expect the village people may have noticed as unfortunately there is a right of way through the churchyard but we cannot think of anywhere else to sit. Is it not curious to think how true it was when I said at the time when you sent me to the Rectory, that you did not realize what you might be expos- ing me to? But now I am so thankful that you did expose me, as I have found my great happiness here, and am so truly happy in a good man's love. Goodbye, I must stop now as the moon has risen and I am just going out to meet Wilfred.

Your loving, full-hearted little niece,

MARIA

Maria, pleased on the whole with this letter, copied it out twice, addressed the neater copy with a flourish, and went to bed. The muslin frills of the nest moved gently on the night air; the moon rose beaming over the churchyard and the pale evening primroses fringing the garden path. No daughter of Mrs Dosely's could have smiled more tenderly in the dark or fallen asleep more innocently.

Mr Hammond had no calendar in his rooms: he was sent so many at Christmas that he threw them all away and was left with none, so he ticked off the days mentally. Three weeks and six long days had still to elapse before the end of Maria's visit. He remained shut up in his rooms for mornings together, to the neglect of the parish, and was supposed to be writing a book on Cardinal Newman. Postcards of arch white kittens stepping through rosy wreaths arrived for him daily; once he had come in to find a cauliflower labelled 'From an admirer' on his sitting room table. Mrs Higgins, the landlady, said the admirer must have come in by the window, as *she* had admitted no one, so recently Mr Hammond lived with his window hasped. This morning, the Saturday after the Choral Society's gala, as he sat humped over his table writing his sermon, a shadow blotted the lower window panes. Maria, obscuring what light there was in the room with her body, could see in only with difficulty; her nose appeared white and flattened; she rolled her eyes ferociously round the gloom. Then she began trying to push the window up.

'*Go away!*' shouted Mr Hammond, waving his arms explosively, as at a cat.

'You must let me in, I have something awful to tell you,' shouted Maria, lips close to the pane. He didn't, so she went round to the front door and was admitted by Mrs Higgins with due ceremony. Mrs Higgins, beaming, ushered in the little lady from the Rectory who had come, she said, with an urgent message from Mrs Dosely.

Maria came in, her scarlet beret tipped up, with the jaunty and gallant air of some young lady intriguing for Bonny Prince Charlie.

'Are we alone?' she said loudly, then waited for Mrs Higgins to shut the door. 'I thought of writing to you,' she continued, 'but your coldness to me lately led me to think that was hopeless.' She hooked her heels on his fender and stood rocking backwards and forwards. 'Mr Hammond, I warn you: you must leave Malton Peele at once.'

'I wish *you* would,' said Mr Hammond, who, seated, looked past her left ear with a calm concentration of loathing.

'I dare say I may,' said Maria, 'but I don't want you to be involved in my downfall. You have your future to think of: you may be a bishop; I am only a woman. You see, the fact is, Mr Hammond, from the way we have been going about together, many people think we must be engaged. I don't want to embarrass you, Mr Hammond.'

Mr Hammond was not embarrassed. 'I always have thought you a horrid little girl, but I never knew you were quite so silly,' he said.

'We've been indiscreet. I don't know what my uncle will say. I only hope you won't be compelled to marry me.'

'Get off that fender,' said Mr Hammond; 'you're ruining it . . . Well then, stay there; I want to look at you. I must say you're something quite new.'

'Yes, aren't I?' said Maria complacently.

'Yes. Any other ugly, insignificant-looking little girls I've known did something to redeem themselves from absolute unattractiveness by being pleasant, say, or a little helpful, or sometimes they were well bred, or had good table manners, or were clever and amusing to talk to. If it were not for the consideration of the Doselys for your unfortunate aunt – who is, I understand from Mr Dosely, so stupid as to be almost mentally deficient – they would keep you – since they really have guaranteed to keep you – in some kind of shed or loose-box at the bottom of the yard . . . I don't want to speak in anger,' went on Mr Hammond, 'I hope I'm not angry; I'm simply sorry for you. I always knew the Doselys took in Anglo-Indian children, but if I'd known they dealt in … cases … of your sort, I doubt if I'd have ever come to Malton Peele – Shut up, you little hell-cat! I'll teach you to pull my hair –'

She was on top of him all at once, tweaking his hair with science.

'You beastly Bolshevik!' exclaimed Maria, tugging. He caught her wrists and held them. 'Oh! Shut up – you hurt me, you beastly bully, you! Oh! how could you hurt a girl!' She kicked at his shin, weeping. 'I – I only came,' she said, 'because I was sorry for you. I needn't have come. And then you go and start beating me up like this – *Ow!*'

'It's your only hope,' said Mr Hammond with a vehement, grave, but very detached expression, twisting her wrist round further. 'Yes, go on, yell – I'm not hurting you. You may be jolly thankful I *am* a curate … As a matter of fact, I got sacked from my prep school for bullying … Odd how these things come back …'

They scuffled. Maria yelped sharply and bit his wrist. 'Ha, you would, would you? … Oh, yes, I know you're a little girl – and a jolly nasty one. The only reason I've ever seen why one wasn't supposed to knock little girls about is that they're generally supposed to be nicer – pleasanter – prettier – than little boys.' He parried a kick and held her at arm's length by her wrists. They glared at each other, both crimson with indignation.

'And you supposed to be a curate!'

'And you supposed to be a lady, you little parasite! This'll teach you – Oh!' said Mr Hammond, sighing luxuriously, 'how pleased the Doselys would be if they knew!'

'Big brute! You great hulking brute!'

'If you'd been my little sister,' said Mr Hammond, regretful, 'this would have happened before. But by this time, of course, you wouldn't be nearly so nasty ... I should chivvy you round the garden and send you up a tree every day.'

'*Socialist!*'

'Well, get along now.' Mr Hammond let go of her wrists. 'You can't go out of the door with a face like that; if you don't want a crowd you'd better go through the window ... Now you run home and snivel to Mrs Dosely.'

'*This* will undo your career,' Maria said, nursing wrists balefully. 'I shall have it put in the papers: BARONET'S NIECE TORTURED BY DEMON CURATE. That will undo your career for you, Mr Hammond.'

'I know, I *know*, but it's worth it!' Mr Hammond exclaimed exaltedly. He was twenty-four, and intensely meant what he said. He pushed up the window. 'Now get out,' he stormed, 'or I'll certainly kick you through it.'

'You are in a kind of a way like a brother to me, aren't you?' remarked Maria, lingering on the sill.

'I am not. Get out!'

'But oh, Mr Hammond, I came here to make a confession. I didn't expect violence, as no one's attacked me before. But I forgive you because it was righteous anger. I'm afraid we *are* rather compromised. You must read this. I posted one just the same to Aunt Ena three days ago.'

Maria handed over the copy of her letter.

'I may be depraved and ugly and bad, but you must admit, Mr Hammond, I'm not stupid.' She watched him read.

Half an hour later Mr Hammond, like a set of walking fire-irons, with Maria, limp as a rag, approached the Rectory. Maria hiccupped and hiccupped; she'd found Mr Hammond had no sense of humour at all. She was afraid he was full of vanity. 'You miserable little liar,' he'd said quite distantly, as though to a slug, and here she was being positively bundled along. If there'd been a scruff to her neck he would have grasped it. Maria had really enjoyed being bullied, but she did hate being despised. Now they were both going into the study to have yet another scene with Mr and Mrs Dosely. She was billed, it appeared, for yet another confession, and she had been so much shaken about that her technique faltered and she couldn't think where to begin. She wondered in a dim way what was going to happen next, and whether Uncle Philip would be coming to find Mr Hammond with a horse-whip.

Mr Hammond was all jaw; he wore a really disagreeable expression. Doris Dosely, up in the drawing room window, gazed with awe for a moment, then disappeared.

'Doris!' yelled Mr Hammond. 'Where is your father? Maria has something to tell him.'

'Dunno,' said Doris, and reappeared in the door. 'But here's a telegram for Maria – mother has opened it: something about a letter.'

'It would be,' said Mr Hammond. 'Give it me here.'

'I can't, I won't,' said Maria, backing away from the telegram. Mr Hammond, gritting his teeth audibly, received the paper from Doris.

YOUR LETTER BLOWN FROM MY HAND OVERBOARD: (he read out) AFTER HAD READ FIRST SENTENCE WILD WITH ANXIETY PLEASE REPEAT CONTENTS BY TELEGRAM YOUR UNCLE PHILIP WISHES YOU JOIN US MARSEILLES WEDNES-DAY AM WRITING DOSELYS AUNT ENA.

'How highly strung poor Lady Rimlade must be,' said Doris kindly.

'She is a better aunt than many people deserve,' said Mr Hammond.

'I think I may feel dull on that dreary old cruise after the sisterly, brotherly family life I've had here,' said Maria wistfully.

★

p. 51—noblesse oblige: *gentry have a duty to serve society.*

p. 55—Maria's apparently innocent question 'Are you a Jesuit?' is 'most unfortunate' because Jesuits are Roman Catholic monks, the furthest imaginable extreme to which Mr Hammond's 'tendencies' might lead.

The plot takes a stock nineteenth-century situation (orphan child taken in by kindly family) which could be expected to turn sentimental (orphan proving suitably meek and grateful) and/or romantic (orphan finally marrying into wealth). But Maria is a twentieth-century girl determined not to become a nineteenth-century cliché. The imaginary engagement of which she writes to Aunt Ena is not romantic at all: she's trying to get herself removed from the kindly family – and also, with incidental spite, to blast Mr Hammond's prospects.

She is defeated by his robust response (a man 'with a jaw'); but also by the author's shameless plot-manipulation (the letter blowing overboard), which chops the story off. (A pity? Might you develop the plot in alternative ways yourself?)

Like the plot, the style also subverts conventional romantic fiction. Whether creating setting or character, a single phrase can make the prose wriggle with life ('alert-looking photographs', 'quite distantly, as though to a slug', 'like a set of walking fire-irons'). But this style is not merely skilfully amusing; its complexity is revealed if we ask ourselves about viewpoint. Who is it who finds the photographs alert-looking, the curtains 'fluttery', and the silver cornets 'spuming' flowers (page 50)? Hardly Maria? Or even Lady Rimlade?

I think the viewpoint at this early moment is that of a sharp-tongued narrator, external to the scene (but not to be confused with the author, who might or might not use this voice in her private life). All stories have narrators, of course; some are characters within them, as in 'The Bewitched Jacket.' But in 'Telling Stories' and 'Dale,' and here in 'Maria,' we have what is called an omniscient (all-knowing) narrator, looking on from outside and able to see into any character's mind. The stories still differ: 'Dale' is told by a chatty townsperson who knows the characters offstage; the narrator of 'Telling Stories' is unobtrusive; while the narrator of 'Maria' seems to pass ironic comments of her own.

Who, I wonder, is thinking, and how seriously, 'It was a really nice school' (p. 51)? Presumably we are hearing Maria's thoughts in 'With inconceivable selfishness' (p. 51)? But in the sentence 'If Mrs Doseley really seemed sympathetic, she thought she might leave the two little dogs with her too' Lady Rimlade is musing quite earnestly: the savage irony is the narrator's. On page 56 'with gratification' and 'incurred' may be the narrator's phrasing, but 'This was not bad for one evening' sounds more like the fifteen-year-old herself. And on page 57 'had managed to see quite a lot of him' is a Maria-like understatement of deadpan innocence which throws us off guard for what follows. This lively interplay of different viewpoints and styles can be studied anywhere in the story.

FOR FURTHER READING:

Anything by Elizabeth Bowen (not mainly a writer of comedy). Her most celebrated novel is *The Death of the Heart*, about growing up in pre-war London.

E. L. DOCTOROW

★

E. L. Doctorow lives and works in New York and is best
known as a novelist.

The Writer in the Family

─────────────────────── ★ ───────────────────────

In 1955 my father died with his ancient mother still alive in a
nursing home. The old lady was ninety and hadn't even
known he was ill. Thinking the shock might kill her, my
aunts told her that he had moved to Arizona for his bronchi-
tis. To the immigrant generation of my grandmother, Arizona
was the American equivalent of the Alps, it was where you
went for your health. More accurately, it was where you went
if you had the money. Since my father had failed in all the
business enterprises of his life, this was the aspect of the news
my grandmother dwelled on, that he had finally had some
success. And so it came about that as we mourned him at
home in our stocking feet, my grandmother was bragging to
her cronies about her son's new life in the dry air of the
desert.

My aunts had decided on their course of action without
consulting us. It meant neither my mother nor my brother
nor I could visit Grandma because we were supposed to have
moved west too, a family, after all. My brother Harold and I
didn't mind – it was always a nightmare at the old people's

66

home, where they all sat around staring at us while we tried to make conversation with Grandma. She looked terrible, had numbers of ailments, and her mind wandered. Not seeing her was no disappointment either for my mother, who had never gotten along with the old woman and did not visit when she could have. But what was disturbing was that my aunts had acted in the manner of that side of the family of making government on everyone's behalf, the true citizens by blood and the lesser citizens by marriage. It was exactly this attitude that had tormented my mother all her married life. She claimed Jack's family had never accepted her. She had battled them for twenty-five years as an outsider.

A few weeks after the end of our ritual mourning my Aunt Frances phoned us from her home in Larchmont. Aunt Frances was the wealthier of my father's sisters. Her husband was a lawyer, and both her sons were at Amherst. She had called to say that Grandma was asking why she didn't hear from Jack. I had answered the phone. 'You're the writer in the family,' my aunt said. 'Your father had so much faith in you. Would you mind making up something? Send it to me and I'll read it to her. She won't know the difference.'

That evening, at the kitchen table, I pushed my homework aside and composed a letter. I tried to imagine my father's response to his new life. He had never been west. He had never travelled anywhere. In his generation the great journey was from the working class to the professional class. He hadn't managed that either. But he loved New York, where he had been born and lived his life, and he was always discovering new things about it. He especially loved the old parts of the city below Canal Street, where he would find ships' chandlers or firms that wholesaled in spices and teas. He was a salesman for an appliance jobber with accounts all over the city. He liked to bring home rare cheeses or exotic foreign vegetables that were sold only in certain neighbourhoods. Once he brought home a barometer, another time an antique ship's telescope in a wooden case with a brass snap.

'Dear Mama,' I wrote. 'Arizona is beautiful. The sun shines all day and the air is warm and I feel better than I have in years. The desert is not as barren as you would expect, but filled with wildflowers and cactus plants and peculiar crooked trees that look like men holding their arms out. You can see great distances in whatever direction you turn and to the west is a range of mountains maybe fifty miles from here, but in the morning with the sun on them you can see the snow on their crests.'

My aunt called some days later and told me it was when she read this letter aloud to the old lady that the full effect of Jack's death came over her. She had to excuse herself and went out in the parking lot to cry. 'I wept so,' she said. 'I felt such terrible longing for him. You're so right, he loved to go places, he loved life, he loved everything.'

We began trying to organize our lives. My father had borrowed money against his insurance and there was very little left. Some commissions were still due but it didn't look as if his firm would honour them. There was a couple of thousand dollars in a savings bank that had to be maintained there until the estate was settled. The lawyer involved was Aunt Frances' husband and he was very proper. 'The estate!' my mother muttered, gesturing as if to pull out her hair. 'The estate!' She applied for a job part-time in the admissions office of the hospital where my father's terminal illness had been diagnosed, and where he had spent some months until they had sent him home to die. She knew a lot of the doctors and staff and she had learned 'from bitter experience' as she told them, about the hospital routine. She was hired.

I hated that hospital, it was dark and grim and full of tortured people. I thought it was masochistic of my mother to seek out a job there, but did not tell her so.

We lived in an apartment on the corner of 175th Street and the Grand Concourse, one flight up. Three rooms. I shared the bedroom with my brother. It was jammed with furniture because when my father had required a hospital bed in the last weeks of his illness we had moved some of the living room pieces into the bedroom and made over the living room for him. We had to navigate bookcases, beds, a gateleg table, bureaus, a record player and radio console, stacks of 78 albums, my brother's trombone and music stand, and so on. My mother continued to sleep on the convertible sofa in the living room that had been their bed before his illness. The two rooms were connected by a narrow hall made even narrower by bookcases along the wall. Off the hall were a small kitchen and dinette and a bathroom. There were lots of appliances in the kitchen – broiler, toaster, pressure cooker, counter-top dishwasher, blender – that my father had gotten through his job, at cost. A treasured phrase in our house: *at cost*. But most of these fixtures went unused because my mother did not care for them. Chromium devices with timers or gauges that required the reading of elaborate instructions were not for her. They were in part responsible for the awful clutter of our lives and now she wanted to get rid of them. 'We're being buried,' she said. 'Who needs them!'

So we agreed to throw out or sell anything inessential. While I found boxes for the appliances and my brother tied the boxes with twine, my mother opened my father's closet and took out his clothes. He had several suits because as a salesman he needed to look his best. My mother wanted us to try on his suits to see which of them could be altered and used. My brother refused to try them on. I tried on one jacket which was too large for me. The lining inside the sleeves chilled my arms and the vaguest scent of my father's being came to me.

'This is way too big,' I said.

'Don't worry,' my mother said. 'I had it cleaned. Would I let you wear it if I hadn't?'

It was the evening, the end of winter, and snow was coming down on the windowsill and melting as it settled. The ceiling bulb glared on a pile of my father's suits and trousers on hangers flung across the bed in the shape of a dead man. We refused to try on anything more, and my mother began to cry.

'What are you crying for?' my brother shouted. 'You wanted to get rid of things, didn't you?'

A few weeks later my aunt phoned again and said she thought it would be necessary to have another letter from Jack. Grandma had fallen out of her chair and bruised herself and was very depressed.

'How long does this go on?' my mother said.

'It's not so terrible,' my aunt said, 'for the little time left to make things easier for her.'

My mother slammed down the phone. 'He can't even die when he wants to!' she cried. 'Even death comes second to Mama! What are they afraid of, the shock will kill her? Nothing can kill her. She's indestructible! A stake through the heart couldn't kill her!'

When I sat down in the kitchen to write the letter I found it more difficult than the first one. 'Don't watch me,' I said to my brother. 'It's hard enough.'

'You don't have to do something just because someone wants you to,' Harold said. He was two years older than me and had started at City College; but when my father became ill he had switched to night school and gotten a job in a record store.

'Dear Mama,' I wrote. 'I hope you're feeling well. We're all fit as a fiddle. The life here is good and the people are very friendly and informal. Nobody wears suits and ties here. Just a pair of slacks and a short-sleeved shirt. Perhaps a sweater in the evening. I have bought into a very successful radio and record business and I'm doing very well. You remember Jack's Electric, my old place on 43rd Street? Well, now it's Jack's Arizona Electric and we have a line of television sets as well.'

I sent that letter off to my Aunt Frances, and as we all knew she would, she phoned soon after. My brother held his hand over the mouthpiece. 'It's Frances with her latest review,' he said.

'Jonathan? You're a very talented young man. I just wanted to tell you what a blessing your letter was. Her whole face lit up when I read the part about Jack's store. That would be an excellent way to continue.'

'Well, I hope I don't have to do this any more, Aunt Frances. It's not very honest.'

Her tone changed. 'Is your mother there? Let me talk to her.'

'She's not here,' I said.

'Tell her not to worry,' my aunt said. 'A poor old lady who has never wished anything but the best for her will soon die.'

I did not repeat this to my mother, for whom it would have been one more in the family anthology of unforgivable remarks. But then I had to suffer it myself for the possible truth it might embody. Each side defended its position with rhetoric, but I, who wanted peace, rationalized the snubs and rebuffs each inflicted on the other, taking no stands, like my father himself.

Years ago his life had fallen into a pattern of business failures and missed opportunities. The great debate between his family on the one side, and my mother Ruth on the other, was this: who was responsible for the fact that he had not lived up to anyone's expectations?

As to the prophecies, when spring came my mother's prevailed. Grandma was still alive.

One balmy Sunday my mother and brother and I took the bus to the Beth El cemetery in New Jersey to visit my father's grave. It was situated on a slight rise. We stood looking over rolling fields embedded with monuments. Here and there processions of black cars wound their way through the lanes, or clusters of people stood at open graves. My father's grave was planted with tiny shoots of evergreen but it lacked a headstone. We had chosen one and paid for it and then the stonecutters had gone on strike. Without a headstone my father did not seem to be honourably dead. He didn't seem to me properly buried.

My mother gazed at the plot beside his, reserved for her coffin. 'They were always too fine for other people,' she said. 'Even in the old days on Stanton Street. They put on airs. Nobody was ever good enough for them. Finally Jack himself was not good enough for them. Except to get them things wholesale. Then he was good enough for them.'

'Mom, please,' my brother said.

'If I had known. Before I ever met him he was tied to his mama's apron strings. And Essie's apron strings were like chains, let me tell you. We had to live where we could be near them for the Sunday visits. Every Sunday, that was my life, a visit to mamaleh. Whatever she knew I wanted, a better apartment, a stick of furniture, a summer camp for the boys, she spoke against it. You know your father, every decision had to be considered and reconsidered. And nothing changed. Nothing ever changed.'

She began to cry. We sat her down on a nearby bench. My brother walked off and read the names on stones. I looked at my mother, who was crying, and I went off after my brother.

'Mom's still crying,' I said. 'Shouldn't we do something?'

'It's all right,' he said. 'It's what she came here for.'

'Yes,' I said, and then a sob escaped from my throat. 'But I feel like crying too.'

My brother Harold put his arm around me. 'Look at this old black stone here,' he said. 'The way it's carved. You can see the changing fashion in monuments – just like everything else.'

Somewhere in this time I began dreaming of my father. Not the robust father of my childhood, the handsome man with healthy pink skin and brown eyes and a moustache and the thinning hair parted in the middle. My dead father. We were taking him home from the hospital. It was understood that he had come back from death. This was amazing and joyous. On the other hand, he was terribly mysteriously damaged, or, more accurately, spoiled and unclean. He was very yellowed and debilitated by his death, and there were no guarantees that he wouldn't soon die again. He seemed aware of this and his entire personality was changed. He was angry and impatient with all of us. We were trying to help him in some way, struggling to get him home, but something prevented us, something we had to fix, a tattered suitcase that had sprung open, some mechanical thing: he had a car but it wouldn't start; or the car was made of wood; or his clothes, which had become too large for him, had caught in the door. In one version he was all bandaged and as we tried to lift him from his wheelchair into a taxi the bandage began to unroll and catch in the spokes of the wheelchair. This seemed to be some unreasonableness on his part. My mother looked on sadly and tried to get him to cooperate.

That was the dream. I shared it with no one. Once when I woke, crying out, my brother turned on the light. He wanted to know what I'd been dreaming but I pretended I didn't remember. The dream made me feel guilty. I felt guilty *in* the dream too because my enraged father knew we didn't want to live with him. The dream represented us taking him home, or trying to, but it was nevertheless understood by all of us that

73

he was to live alone. He was this derelict back from death, but what we were doing was taking him to some place where he would live by himself without help from anyone until he died again.

At one point I became so fearful of this dream that I tried not to go to sleep. I tried to think of good things about my father and to remember him before his illness. He used to call me 'matey'. 'Hello, matey,' he would say when he came home from work. He always wanted us to go someplace – to the store, to the park, to a ball game. He loved to walk. When I went walking with him he would say: 'Hold your shoulders back, don't slump. Hold your head up and look at the world. Walk as if you meant it!' As he strode down the street his shoulders moved from side to side, as if he was hearing some kind of cakewalk. He moved with a bounce. He was always eager to see what was around the corner.

The next request for a letter coincided with a special occasion in the house: my brother Harold had met a girl he liked and had gone out with her several times. Now she was coming to our house for dinner.

We had prepared for this for days, cleaning everything in sight, giving the house a going-over, washing the dust of disuse from the glasses and good dishes. My mother came home early from work to get the dinner going. We opened the gateleg table in the living room and brought in the kitchen chairs. My mother spread the table with a laundered white cloth and put out her silver. It was the first family occasion since my father's illness.

I liked my brother's girlfriend a lot. She was a thin girl with very straight hair and she had a terrific smile. Her presence seemed to excite the air. It was amazing to have a living breathing girl in our house. She looked around and what she said was: 'Oh, I've never seen so many books!'

While she and my brother sat at the table my mother was in the kitchen putting the food into serving bowls and I was going from the kitchen to the living room, kidding around like a waiter, with a white cloth over my arm and a high style of service, placing the serving dish of green beans on the table with a flourish. In the kitchen my mother's eyes were sparkling. She looked at me and nodded and mimed the words: 'She's adorable!'

My brother suffered himself to be waited on. He was wary of what we might say. He kept glancing at the girl – her name was Susan – to see if we met with her approval. She worked in an insurance office and was taking courses in accounting at City College. Harold was under a terrible strain but he was excited and happy too. He had bought a bottle of Concord-grape wine to go with the roast chicken. He held up his glass and proposed a toast. My mother said: 'To good health and happiness,' and we all drank, even I. At that moment the phone rang and I went into the bedroom to get it.

'Jonathan? This is your Aunt Frances. How is everyone?'

'Fine, thank you.'

'I want to ask one last favour of you. I need a letter from Jack. Your grandma's very ill. Do you think you can?'

'Who is it?' my mother called from the living room,.

'OK, Aunt Frances,' I said quickly. 'I have to go now, we're eating dinner.' And I hung up the phone.

'It was my friend Louie,' I said, sitting back down. 'He didn't know the math pages to review.'

The dinner was very fine. Harold and Susan washed the dishes and by the time they were done my mother and I had folded up the gateleg table and put it back against the wall and I had swept the crumbs up with the carpet sweeper. We all sat and talked and listened to records for a while and then my brother took Susan home. The evening had gone very well.

Once when my mother wasn't home my brother had pointed out something: the letters from Jack weren't really necessary. 'What is this ritual?' he said, holding his palms up. 'Grandma is almost totally blind, she's half deaf and crippled. Does the situation really call for a literary composition? Does it need verisimilitude? Would the old lady know the difference if she was read the phone book?'

'Then why did Aunt Frances ask me?'

'That is the question, Jonathan. Why did she? After all, she could write the letter herself – what difference would it make? And if not Frances, why not Frances' sons, the Amherst students? They should have learned by now to write.'

'But they're not Jack's sons,' I said.

'That's exactly the point,' my brother said. 'The idea is *service*. Dad used to bust his balls getting them things wholesale, getting them deals on things. Frances of Westchester really needed things at cost. And Aunt Molly. And Aunt Molly's husband, and Aunt Molly's ex-husband. Grandma, if she needed an errand done. He was always on the hook for something. They never thought his time was important. They never thought every favour he got was one he had to pay back. Appliances, records, watches, china, opera tickets, any goddamn thing. Call Jack."

'It was a matter of pride to him to be able to do things for them,' I said. 'To have connections.'

'Yeah, I wonder why,' my brother said. He looked out the window.

Then suddenly it dawned on me that I was being implicated.

'You should use your head more,' my brother said.

Yet I had agreed once again to write a letter from the desert and so I did. I mailed it off to Aunt Frances. A few days later, when I came home from school, I thought I saw her sitting in her car in front of our house. She drove a black Buick Roadmaster, a very large clean car with whitewall tires. It was Aunt Frances all right. She blew the horn when she saw me. I went over and leaned in at the window.

'Hello, Jonathan,' she said. 'I haven't long. Can you get in the car?'

'Mom's not home,' I said. 'She's working.'

'I know that. I came to talk to you.'

'Would you like to come upstairs?'

'I can't, I have to get back to Larchmont. Can you get in for a moment, please?'

I got in the car. My Aunt Frances was a very pretty white-haired woman, very elegant, and she wore tasteful clothes. I had always liked her and from the time I was a child she had enjoyed pointing out to everyone that I looked more like her son than Jack's. She wore white gloves and held the steering wheel and looked straight ahead as she talked, as if the car was in traffic and not sitting at the kerb.

'Jonathan,' she said, 'there is your letter on the seat. Needless to say I didn't read it to Grandma. I'm giving it back to you and I won't ever say a word to anyone. This is just between us. I never expected cruelty from you. I never thought you were capable of doing something so deliberately cruel and perverse.'

I said nothing.

'Your mother has very bitter feelings and now I see she has poisoned you with them. She has always resented the family. She is a very strong-willed, selfish person.'

'No she isn't,' I said.

'I wouldn't expect you to agree. She drove poor Jack crazy with her demands. She always had the highest aspirations and he could never fulfil them to her satisfaction. When he still had his store he kept your mother's brother, who drank,

77

on salary. After the war when he began to make a little money he had to buy Ruth a mink jacket because she was so desperate to have one. He had debts to pay but she wanted a mink. He was a very special person, my brother, he should have accomplished something special, but he loved your mother and devoted his life to her. And all she ever thought about was keeping up with the Joneses.'

I watched the traffic going up the Grand Concourse. A bunch of kids were waiting at the bus stop at the corner. They had put their books on the ground and were horsing around.

'I'm sorry I have to descend to this,' Aunt Frances said. 'I don't like talking about people this way. If I have nothing good to say about someone, I'd rather not say anything. How is Harold?'

'Fine.'

'Did he help you write this marvellous letter?'

'No.'

After a moment she said more softly: 'How are you all getting along?'

'Fine.'

'I would invite you up for Passover if I thought your mother would accept.'

I didn't answer.

She turned on the engine. 'I'll say goodbye now, Jonathan. Take your letter. I hope you give some time to thinking about what you've done.'

That evening when my mother came home from work I saw that she wasn't as pretty as my Aunt Frances. I usually thought my mother was a good-looking woman, but I saw now that she was too heavy and that her hair was undistinguished.

'Why are you looking at me?' she said.

'I'm not.'

'I learned something interesting today,' my mother said. 'We may be eligible for a VA pension because of the time your father spent in the Navy.'

That took me by surprise. Nobody had ever told me my father was in the Navy.

'In World War I,' she said, 'he went to Webb's Naval Academy on the Harlem River. He was training to be an ensign. But the war ended and he never got his commission.'

After dinner the three of us went through the closets looking for my father's papers, hoping to find some proof that could be filed with the Veterans' Administration. We came up with two things, a Victory medal, which my brother said everyone got for being in the service during the Great War, and an astounding sepia photograph of my father and his shipmates on the deck of a ship. They were dressed in bell-bottoms and T-shirts and armed with mops and pails, brooms and brushes.

'I never knew this,' I found myself saying. 'I never knew this.'

'You just don't remember,' my brother said.

I was able to pick out my father. He stood at the end of the row, a thin, handsome boy with a full head of hair, a moustache, and an intelligent, smiling countenance.

'He had a joke,' my mother said. 'They called their training ship the ss *Constipation* because it never moved.'

Neither the picture nor the medal was proof of anything, but my brother thought a duplicate of my father's service record had to be in Washington somewhere and that it was just a matter of learning how to go about finding it.

'The pension wouldn't amount to much,' my mother said. 'Twenty or thirty dollars. But it would certainly help.'

I took the picture of my father and his shipmates and propped it against the lamp at my bedside. I looked into his youthful face and tried to relate it to the father I knew. I looked at the picture a long time. Only gradually did my eye connect it to the set of Great Sea Novels in the bottom shelf of the bookcase a few feet away. My father had given that set to me: it was uniformly bound in green with gilt lettering and it included works by Melville, Conrad, Victor Hugo and Captain Marryat. And lying across the top of the books, jammed in under the sagging shelf above, was his old ship's telescope in its wooden case with the brass snap.

I thought how stupid, and imperceptive, and self-centred I had been never to have understood while he was alive what my father's dream for his life had been.

On the other hand, I had written in my last letter from Arizona – the one that had so angered Aunt Frances – something that might allow me, the writer in the family, to soften my judgement of myself. I will conclude by giving the letter here in its entirety.

Dear Mama,

This will be my final letter to you since I have been told by the doctors that I am dying.

I have sold my store at a very fine profit and am sending Frances a check for five thousand dollars to be deposited in your account. My present to you, Mamaleh. Let Frances show you the passbook.

As for the nature of my ailment, the doctors haven't told me what it is, but I know that I am simply dying of the wrong life. I should never have come to the desert. It wasn't the place for me.

I have asked Ruth and the boys to have my body cremated and the ashes scattered in the ocean.

Your loving son,
Jack

Because real life is complicated, we give each other simplified accounts of it – for example, if asked about a relative's life, or indeed our own. It has been said that we tell ourselves stories to make sense of our lives – and even when we don't intend to deceive, those versions are inevitably shaped, stylized, their loose ends being tucked away. Even autobiography and history have much in common with fiction.

Our discovery of our parents goes through gradual processes of adjustment (as we learn more of their lives, in different story-versions). And the images we form of them affect our image of ourselves: we may feel that we carry our parents within us. Later, the same may happen in reverse: parents may judge their own success in life by the success of their children.

Here, Aunt Frances presumptuously decides that Grandma should be denied information about something as major as her son's death, and invents the move to Arizona. Grandma herself promptly improves on this story, making it her son's first success in life. The 'writer', Jonathan, is presented with this script outline and has to work to it.

He tries 'to imagine my father's response to his new life': this is a serious task, trying to remember and know his dead father – and then feel on his behalf. On the final page he criticizes himself for not having known his father better – but is relieved to find one detail which seems to have slipped subconsciously into his final fictional letter. (Which detail?)

Meanwhile we hear other versions of the dead man – from Aunt Frances, Mother, Harold, and Aunt Frances again: can you locate them? Each of these characters briefly becomes a narrator, and gives Jack's life a different plot. The Naval record, finally, presents another version. And we have two symbolic episodes – the sons being asked to try on their father's clothing, and Jonathan's repeated and 'guilty' dream in which 'we didn't want to live with him.'

The style is simple, appropriate to the straightforwardness of the boy Jonathan, who wants to be 'honest'; but within it Doctorow draws out much psychological complexity.

FOR FURTHER READING:

E L Doctorow: *Ragtime* (novel); *Lives of the Poets* (stories, of which this is the first, linked together in the final piece). Published by Picador.

JESSE HILL FORD

★

Jesse Hill Ford writes about Tennessee, a relatively backward rural area of the USA. Jake, the narrator of this story, comes from Texas, many hundreds of miles away: by 'natives' he means the Tennessee hillbilly (white) people.

The Surest Thing in Show Business

———————————————— ★ ————————————————

Things didn't pan out in Texas, so my wife, Jerry, and me, we come East in our old car, hauling a trailer loaded with three hundred pounds of snakes, an old cheetah, and a bear cub. We found this place we could rent on the highway, just outside the Great Smoky Mountains National Park, on the Tennessee side, so we decided to give her a try. It had a large clear space for parking and was on a long mountain grade going into the Smokies. A long grade that way will get you traffic that stops because the motor gets overheated, and then too, the kids will be yelling they want to see the snakes. So between the radiator and the kids, Daddy, he can't do nothing but stop.

Jerry, my wife, she helped me paint the signs, thirty-nine of them, all bright yellow and red enough to dazzle your eyes, and we tacked them up for two miles along the road on either side of the place, but mostly on the down-grade side. I was able to pick up three fair-size iguana lizards and a couple of

83

pretty good Gila monsters from other reptile folks passing through on the way to Florida, and by the time traffic started really coming through in June, Jerry and me had a nice palisade wall, an admission booth, a free ice-water fountain, a free radiator water tank, and a Cherokee squaw named Lizzie who held down the candy, cigarettes and souvenir stand.

Lizzie was OK, only she cussed and swore when she got excited, which had got her fired from her job at a souvenir joint inside the park. And, too, she was somewhat of a problem at first because she wanted to call me a swear word, and I don't like to have nobody but myself to swear around Jerry. What Lizzie called me sounded like *sumitch,* all one word: 'Gimme some change for this goddam drawer, sumitch.' She wouldn't call me by my own name, Jake, so finally we hit on a sort of middle bargain. 'How's about just calling me Mitch?' I says. And after some practice it worked out OK, and that's how come we changed the name to Mitch and Jerry's Reptile Show in place of Jake and Jerry's. For in show business you got to be ready to wheel and deal and bargain a little if you make it. And any show around the Smokies that don't have at least one real Indian is like a kite without no tail.

By July we was going full blast, and I had took on an old man and a boy to milk a couple of afternoons a week so I could tend to building more animal cages and ordering hot snakes in place of the old ones we brought with us. The old man couldn't do no more than hang a snake's mouth over a milk jar and grin – I mean he didn't actually milk out no venom and never learned – but he had a good line of gab and always drank a little dab of coloured water he hid in the jar ahead of time, and the crowd liked him. Another thing, the old man put on he was more feeble than he really was and made his hands look real shaky so they figured he was going

84

to get bit any second. And that's the whole secret. You go in there to make them believe you might get bit. But now the kid, he milked good and he handled them good and took all kinds of chances, but he made it look too easy and he never got the attention the old man did. The kid never got the point that you can't make it look too easy.

So on the Fourth of July the stranger showed up, one of those long pale guys in a shiny blue suit too small for him, wearing shoes that were never meant for walking – the pointed kind that might have been yellow when they were new – and of course he had walked about a hundred miles. He stayed around the Cherokee's counter for about two hours until she told him to get the hell away from there. Then he hung back a little distance like a stray dog and just stared and waited. Then about noon he got some free ice water and hiked on and I just wrote him off my mind like a bad debt and patted myself on the back for having got a smart Indian out front like Lizzie, even if it did mean changing my handle a little bit. About four o'clock that afternoon he was back. He marched right up to the ticket window like he had money and asked Jerry, my wife, if the boss was around. He didn't need to explain that he was down on his luck. I guess the thing was that he had a Texas drawl and an unexpected soft voice. All of those fellows' voices will startle you, though. The voice never sounds like the guy looks. It's the road that does it. Jerry just pointed at the palisade gate with her thumb, and he slipped right on in on me. I could hear Lizzie swearing when he opened the gate. You would have thought some of the animals was loose. But Lizzie didn't have no use for white men in any form or fashion, especially his kind. They don't take too kindly to walking tourists up in the Smokies, for the walking ones never want to buy nothing and are always looking to put an honest Indian out of her job.

He come in and closed the gate behind him and give a

sidelong glance at the cheetah, which was napping on his sawdust bed in one corner of his cage. I was just through with the three-thirty show and was trying to make a six-foot diamondback get on in his box. He was a new snake and was still hot as hell. I just kept coaxing him with my snake hook and holding that tail, and the other guy waited real polite till I had the diamondback in the box.

'Well?' I says. He was a pitiful sight. With everything else he had a blond moustache. It made him look like the next rain would dissolve him. But then he spoke up, brighter and more eager than I looked for.

'I need a stake,' he says, waving one long hand like he was fending gnats away from his eyes. They were bright and yellow, like the Western sun, and Texas was right there in his voice so that he got to me fast, like remembering home and the old folks. But us show people are soft-hearted anyway.

'I found a little hick place over the ridge there,' he went on, 'talked them out of the high school auditorium for this evening to do a reptile show.' The hand went hunting down into his pocket, the back pants pocket of the blue suit, and I couldn't hardly believe my eyes when it came out again. 'I already collected fifty dollars in advance.' He unfolded the bills one right after the other on top of the glass reptile case at his elbow. The snakes raised up and rattled a little and then laid right back down. They were the last of that original three hundred pounds, and they were getting wore out in a hurry. The most of them don't live over six weeks.

'Hey,' I says, 'I'd call that a pretty good stake already.'

'Yeah,' he says, 'only I ain't got any snakes.'

And there it was. He had located a school and store and a clump of houses up there on the edge of the park, and in three hours he had to be back up there ready to put on a full-feathered reptile show and he didn't have so much as a frog in his pocket. It wasn't any wonder to me at all, because if

I've learned one thing after twenty-five years in show business, it's the fact that there ain't a single living American that ain't had a great-granddaddy or a step-uncle or some connection like that who was swallered whole by a rattler. Understand, they never *knew* him, but Granny told them about it, which makes the rattlesnake the surest moneymaker in American show business. They will pay to see what swallered Grand-daddy everytime. Of course you have to expect the comments. If you have an eight-foot snake – it's another story, but me and my brothers did have one once, a Florida diamondback, and we was so scared of him that we would have almost rather been shot at than to work him. It took three of us to handle him, and never a show went by that some smart bastard didn't pipe up and remark how he killed 'em bigger than that with his bare feet every morning, right by his kitchen door. 'You call *that* a snake?' they yell. But then that's part of why they pay, and in show business you got to roll with the punches.

So he just stood there with the money laid out on the glass over them dying snakes, and I finally says, 'And they even let you leave with the money.'

'Yeah. I told them my truck was broke down and I had to get it fixed before I could bring up my reptiles.'

'When is the show for?' I says.

'Seven o'clock,' he says, 'in the Hartsville High audi-torium.'

'You handled reptiles much?' I says.

'You bet your boots. Hell, it's practically all I ever done.'

'You want hot snakes?' I says. There was two kinds, the fresh hot ones, straight up from the Mexican border and feisty as a coon dog pup, and the old ones, so weak you couldn't hardly put them into a coil unless you just took and wound them up like a piece of old rope.

'Whatever you can spare. Snakes, lizards, anything you can

87

lend me. I'm willing to pay. The money's right there,' he says, tossing his long sand-coloured hair out away from those eyes where it had drooped while he was looking down.

The crowd was grouping up real nice about the arena next to us. I could see the glare off the white sand floor lighting their faces. I took a red balloon out of my pocket and blew it up and tied it. Then I stepped out into the middle of the arena and let it drift down on to the sand floor. Their eyes all went after it like a bunch of bees swarming with their mother queen. 'Now folks, the show starts in just a few minutes,' I says. Nothing can get quiet so quick as a crowd around a snake arena.

Then a kid yells: 'Where are the snakes?'

'Now just be patient, Sonny, I'll be rounding up the stars of the show right away,' I says, and this woman give a hysterical laugh, something like a coyote, and I ducked back into the reptile shed. The stranger had put one of the hot snakes into a coil, a four-foot Mexican green rattler.

'Now there's a hot one, ain't he?' I says, trying to cheer him up.

'Yeah,' he says, 'he's a jim-dandy.' He turned his eyes on me and brushed his hair back from his forehead. 'How much?' he says.

'I ain't going to charge you nothing,' I says. 'I know what it's like to be down.'

'Well say, that's mighty swell. I ain't no beggar, understand.'

'Naw,' I says, 'I'm glad to do it. Only thing, I don't see how I could get anything over there to you much before seven thirty, daylight lasting like it does now. But if seven thirty won't be too late, I'll box up some stuff and hustle it over to the schoolhouse for you in my car. How's that sound?'

'I can hold them thirty minutes easy.'

'Well, I got to get started. This here is a continuous show all afternoon, so I'll see you at half past seven.'

'Couldn't be better,' he says. 'Mind if I watch your act?'

'Help yourself,' I says. I saw him sticking his money back into that rear pants pocket as I picked up my snake box. I left him there in the shed and stepped back into the arena and put my box down. They were still watching the balloon. I took out my snakes and put them each one in a coil by slapping my foot down at them, making a semi-circle of coiled rattlers and starting my spiel. I looked up and saw he had elbowed his way to the rail. When I looked up the next time he was gone.

Before the milking act I took out one of my new iguana lizards. You got to be careful about how you hold an iguana because he's got a bite like a bulldog. The only difference is he don't give you no warning first, no growl, no frown, no hiss. He don't even quiver his eyes or show his tongue before he bites the very *bee*-devil right out of you. I held his head with all the iron I could get into my grip, and when I was done I took out a Gila monster. The old Gila was strong as a young steer. I held him the same way because a Gila is just like an iguana, only worse – once he gets his fangs into you he starts chewing like you was a plug of tobacco or something and you haven't got no alternative but to cut his head off to get him aloose. By then you're poisoned sure enough. So I was glad when I had worked the lizards and got them back in the box. I announced the milking act, and the old man came stumbling out with the kid right behind him and damned near scared the crowd to death. The kid brought the little milking table with the cocktail glass clamped to it, and I milked one and the old man did one, or made out like he did, and then I squirted a little stream of it right out in the air, just to prove to them it was real, squirted it right out of the snake's fang and got another coyote laugh out of the woman.

I had just turned around when the old man started to howl and stuck his hand in his mouth. The crowd laughed some because they all thought it was a phony. They always think the real thing is phony, but I didn't even have to look at his hand to know it was real. The old man's face looked like a batch of cold grits at four a.m.

'Oscar,' I says to the kid, quiet-like, 'drive him to the hospital and don't worry about blowing out no tyres.' They went out and directly I heard the car take off outside and I had lost my best helper, probably for the rest of the season. I had it to myself for the rest of the afternoon, for when Oscar come back from the hospital he was too shaky to do nothing but stand around trembling like a tramp in January. He said the old man was in awful shape, that he was having a rigor and they had cut his arm open and all. 'Don't tell me about it,' I says. 'I've been bit before.' But he kept on, which is the trouble with them natives in the Smokies, that they can't shut up once they get shook. So finally I had to either tell him to go home or get my own self bit just to get away from him. So on the Fourth of July, like it will always happen in show business, I lost my extra help and had to clean out the cheetah's cage and tend to the armadillos all by myself and doctor the bear cub's paw where some tourist had give him a lighted cigar, until I was plumb whipped.

If Jerry, my wife, hadn't asked what that guy wanted I guess I would have forgotten him all the way. As it was I didn't start putting anything in the boxes until seven thirty, and then it was harum-scarum. I just grabbed up the first things I could lay my hands on and marked the cardboard boxes on the lids. Since I hadn't had no assistants to go behind the crowd and start them clapping, there hadn't been no applause all afternoon and Jerry could see I was whipped out. It's that applause that keeps you going in show business anyway. I went on marking the boxes, and Jerry says, 'I hope he realizes what a favour you're doing him, after what all happened. You look wore out, Jake.'

'Look,' I says, 'will you just start putting these here boxes in the car? I promised him seven thirty. He's up there on the ridge now trying to hold his audience.' I was in a hurry, so I just put on MG for Mexican green and TDB for Texas diamond-back and G for Gila monster and so on, right on the top where he could read it before he took the lid off. I took the hottest stuff we had and piled it in the back seat and grabbed a snake hook and we took off, me and my wife, Jerry, fast as the old car would run. The last word the Cherokee yelled when we left was one I don't like to hear said around Jerry. I could tell that Indian squaw was against us giving any helping hand to a walking tourist. 'He had a nice way of talking,' Jerry said while we rolled up the mountain. 'Texas,' I said back to her and reached out for her little hand and gave it a big squeeze.

I guess it was eight o'clock anyway before we got to the schoolhouse, and he had crowded more natives into it than I would have thought was staked out in all them hills. Not only that but they were waiting just as faithful and polite as a bunch of treed house cats. A few had stood up and were jawing a little, but when Jerry and I came in they sneaked on back and sat down like they was trained that way.

The reason was right up there on the Hartsville High School auditorium stage, and when he opened his mouth it wasn't any wonder. If his spiel was a little wild, it was anyway one of the best I ever heard. Before Jerry and I could get the car unloaded and get the boxes on the stage, he had me believing I really was his 'assistant', as he called me. Not only that, me and Jerry both hurried whenever we went out to the car for more boxes, so we wouldn't miss too much of what he said in his introduction. It wasn't any question but what he was good. And every time I took him a box on to the stage I tried to take him aside to explain about the markings on top, and every time he gave me the most elegant my-good-man treatment, waving me off and telling me where to set the box, until I just finally gave up.

I'll say this much for him. He did save us two seats down front which I appreciated, for I was in a notion to have a little nap during the show. In fact, if somebody had of told me anything could keep me awake, I would of laughed. But we hadn't sat down good and I hadn't closed my eyes quite shut, listening to him run on about Africa and Tibet and Peru and Norway and jungles and all, until Jerry's elbow, which is a sharp little thing, come into my side like a pool cue. I snapped open my eyes and started to say something rough to her, and then I looked at the stage and swallered my words whole. For he had put a Mexican green rattler into a coil and set a four-bit piece on its head. I heard him say it three times: 'Now folks, I'm going to push that fifty cents off on the floor with my nose.'

'Aw, why don't he *do* something,' the woman on the other side of me says.

Jerry had hid her face against my shoulder. There just wasn't no way for the Mexican green to miss hitting him in the face. I figured we wouldn't get him outdoors until he'd be dead. And there his crowd was, already bitching and griping and him up on the stage like somebody bobbing apples without no tub, right over that snake's head, and it rattling so fast it was singing. He was doing a stunt that I had not seen or heard of, and which I knew I would not ever see again. In show business you always save your best stunt until last, and so I knew then what he was and where he had probably escaped from. It was the kind of stunt to end your life, instead of your act. I kept wondering if he had got the idea somewhere that their fangs had all been pulled out. The snake missed him three times and three times he put his four-bit piece back on its head. The last time he got his nose down and pushed the money off. By then it had sort of got through to the crowd what he was up to, and when that money hit the floor the last time, you could hear it roll. Then the snake struck and missed. It struck right through his hair, where it was hanging down, and I saw him brush it back with that quick flip of his head. He started up his spiel again, and I started wondering if maybe he used his hair that way on purpose. I didn't have to wait long. He was talking and opening boxes and the snakes were getting out mostly by themselves. Sometimes he stomped at them and put them in a coil, and other times he just let them come on out like they would or even dumped them. Then he reached in a box and hauled out the iguana by its tail. He held it up right in front of his face and laughed.

'Folks,' he says, 'I'm going to be honest with you. I don't know what this thing is.' It was the truth, because he scratched it on the head. I kept waiting to hear him scream. But the iguana just hung there like he was in a tree at home and let that guy do anything he pleased.

Then he found the Gila monster. 'Now,' he says, 'I do know what this here one is. This here is a Gila monster.'

He handled it like it was stuffed and had its jaws wired. In fact he sort of waved it about while his spiel went on. I could feel my heart jumping, and Jerry's fingernails dug into my arm until it was starting to get numb. 'You've heard lots of folks say Gila monsters is poison? Well, my friends, this little old lizard is not poison at all. People have told a lie on him all these years, and this evening I'm going to prove it to you. I'm going to show you he's ab-so-lute-ly harmless. Yes, friends and neighbours, I want you to watch me now. I'm going to stick my own tongue into this little feller's mouth.'

'Anybody knows *they* ain't poison,' the woman next to me says. 'He sure is a gyp, ain't he?'

'Well, what did you expect?' says her old man.

It's the only time I ever left Jerry alone like that since we been married, but I just took her fingers aloose. 'You ain't leaving?' she says.

'Yes,' I says. 'I'll be just outside if you need me.'

'I'll holler for you when the monster latches on,' she says.

'No need,' I says. 'I ain't going more than a mile. I'll hear him okay.'

There was several guffaws as I walked out and I turned just once to look, and sure enough, he had that lizard up and was trying to poke his tongue in its mouth. I just hurried on outside and leaned up against the wall of the school building, feeling dizzy. I felt to make sure I had my pocketknife. Somebody would have to catch him and hold him while I cut the lizard's head off and then prized it off his tongue. I didn't know if I'd be up to it, and it was right there, the first time, that I wondered if I could stay on with show business. Inside they was busting gussets in all directions, laughing like a bunch of stooges. Then I heard his spiel again and risked a look inside the door. He had put the Gila monster up and was moving into something else. He had put a Texas diamond-back around his neck like a scarf. I went on back in and sat down by Jerry.

'Everybody knows he's yanked the teeth out of every last one of them pore varmints,' the woman by me says. 'A fake, that's all in the world he is.'

'What happened?' I says to Jerry.

'He couldn't make the lizard open its mouth,' she says.

After a few more things, like milking venom straight into his mouth, he wound up his show and Jerry and I started the applause. It was kind of seedy. I didn't say anything. I just helped get everything off the stage and back into the boxes. Then we loaded the car and he crawled in the back seat instead of sitting up front like I asked him, and we started back down the mountain. I figured he wanted to get in the back so he could pet the iguana some more. Anyway I was too sore at him to say anything for a while. Finally I asked him what his name was.

'Doug,' he says.

'Where did you say you worked reptiles before, Doug?' I says.

'I ain't going to lie to you,' he says. I guess he thought it over then, for he paused before he finally said the truth. 'Tonight was my first time,' he says.

And then he told us he had worked around oil fields mostly and was just coming East when he saw our place there on the road and saw Lizzie behind the souvenir counter. I felt like stopping the car right there and kicking him off the side of the ridge, but in my business you can't always yield to temptation and make a go of it. I had to bear in mind that the old man was in the hospital snake-bit and Oscar was so shell-shocked over it there was no telling when *he* could go back to milking again. So I waited awhile until I could get a hold on myself. We passed the first one of our signs. It drifted by in the headlights. 'Doug,' I says, soft as I could manage, 'how would you like to learn the reptile business?'

'By gummy, Mitch,' he says, 'I was hoping you would ask me that.'

The first-person viewpoint here is essential to the story's effect on us: why? Think, for example, of the moment when the old man is bitten, or of the audience reactions in the high-school auditorium. The true plot and drama are known only to Jake and Jerry, and therefore to us: everyone else remains cheerfully unaware.

What stylistic touches help us to feel that Jake is really talking to us? Look at his incidental comments, and the instinctive comparisons he uses.

This speaking voice helps to give a feeling of authenticity. So do the technical details of snake-handling, and the vividness of setting and atmosphere – 'the glare off the white sand floor lighting their faces', the snakes rising up and rattling when Doug puts his money on their glass case, the sound of the 50-cent piece rolling across the stage. Finally, the story is rich in characters: what might have been a mere yarn becomes much fuller and warmer by the inclusion of Lizzie, Oscar, the old man, the woman with the coyote laugh and the scoffing woman in the auditorium, as well as, of course, the movie-like figure of the Texan lone stranger.

FOR FURTHER READING:

Fishes, Birds and Sons of Men: stories by Jesse Hill Ford (Bodley Head).

PRIMO LEVI

Primo Levi (1919–1987) was an Italian scientist. As a Jew
resisting Italian fascism and German Nazism, he was deported
during the Second World War to Auschwitz concentration
camp, from which he was one of very few to survive. After
the war he returned to his work as a chemist, but also became
well known as a writer, both for his accounts of Auschwitz
and for his fiction – though the story here (a scientist's
science fiction) was first published under a pen-name. It is
translated by Raymond Rosenthal.

Order on the Cheap

I am always pleased to see Mr Simpson. He's not one of your
usual salesmen, who remind me of public defenders: he's
truly in love with the NATCA machines, believes in them with
innocent faith, torments himself over their flaws and break-
downs, triumphs with their triumphs. Or at least, that's how
he seems to be, even if he is not – which, to all intents and
purposes, amounts to the same thing.

Even leaving aside our business relations, we're almost
friends; nevertheless, I had lost sight of him in 1960
after he sold me the Versifier: he was terribly busy, filling the
demands for that very successful model, working every day
until midnight. Then, toward the middle of August, he had

phoned to ask me whether I was interested in a Turbo confessor: a fast, portable model very much in demand in America and approved by Cardinal Spellman. I wasn't interested and I told him so quite bluntly.

A few months ago Mr Simpson rang my doorbell unannounced. He was radiant and in his arms, with the fondness of a nanny, he carried a box of corrugated cardboard. He wasted no time on conventionalities: 'Here it is,' he said triumphantly. 'It's the Mimer: the duplicator we've all dreamt about.'

'A duplicator?' I said, barely able to conceal a gesture of disappointment. 'Sorry, Simpson, I never dreamt about duplicators. How could anything be better than the ones we've got? Look here, for example. Five cents and in a few seconds a copy, and they are irreproachable copies; dry processing, no reactive agents, not even a single breakdown in two years.'

But Mr Simpson wasn't easy to deflate. 'If you'll forgive me, anyone can reproduce a surface. This reproduces not just the surface but also in depth'; and with a politely hurt expression he added, 'The Mimer is a *true* duplicator.' From his attaché case he cautiously drew two stencilled sheets with coloured headings and placed them on the table. 'Which is the original?'

I examined them attentively; yes, they were the same, but weren't two copies of the same newspaper, two prints from the same negative, equally the same?

'No, look more closely. You see, for this demonstration material we've deliberately chosen a coarse paper, with many extraneous elements in the pulp. Furthermore, we tore this corner deliberately before duplication. Get a magnifying glass and take your time examining it. I'm in no hurry – this afternoon is devoted to you.'

At one spot on one of the copies there was a fleck, and next to it a yellow grain; at the same position on the second copy there was a fleck and a yellow grain. The two tears were identical, down to the last tiny speck that could be distinguished through the glass. My scepticism was being transformed into curiosity.

Meanwhile Mr Simpson had pulled from his case an entire file. 'This is my ammunition,' he said to me smiling, with his pleasant foreign accent. 'It's my support group of twins.' There were handwritten letters, underlined at random in various colours; envelopes with stamps; complicated technical drawings; varicoloured childish doodlings. Of each specimen Mr Simpson showed me the exact replica, both front and back.

I carefully examined the demonstration material: it was in truth totally satisfactory. The grain of the paper, every mark, every shading of colour, were reproduced with absolute fidelity. I noticed that the same rough spots found on the originals were to be found on the copies: the greasiness of the crayon lines, the chalky dryness of the highlights in the tempera background, the embossment of the stamps. Meanwhile Mr Simpson continued his pitch. 'This is not an improvement on a previous model: the very principle on which the Mimer is based is revolutionary, extremely interesting not only from a practical point of view but also conceptually. It does not imitate, it does not simulate, but rather it reproduces the model, re-creates it identically, so to speak, from nothing . . .'

I gave a start: my chemist's viscera protested violently against such an enormity. 'Really! How from nothing?'

'Forgive me if I've let myself be carried away. Not just from nothing, obviously. I meant to say from chaos, from absolute disorder. There, that's what the Mimer does: it creates order from disorder.'

He went out to the street and from the trunk of his car took a small metal cylinder, not unlike a container of liquid gas. He showed me how, by means of a flexible tube, it should be connected with the Mimer's cell.

'This is the fuel tank. It contains a rather complex blend, the so-called pabulum whose nature for the time being is under wraps; based on what I think I understood from the technicians at NATCA during the training course at Fort Kiddiwanee, it is likely that the pabulum is made up of not very stable composites of carbon and of other principal vital elements ... The procedure is elementary: between you, me and the lamp-post I really haven't understood why it was necessary to call all of us to America from the four corners of the world. Now look, you put the model to be reproduced in this compartment and in this other compartment, which is identical in shape and volume, you introduce the pabulum at a controlled velocity. During the duplication process, in the exact position of every single atom of the model is fixed an analogous atom extracted from the alimentation mixture: carbon where there was carbon, nitrogen where there was nitrogen, and so on. Naturally, we salesmen have been told almost nothing about the mechanism of this long-distance reconstruction, nor have we been told in what way the enormous bulk of information at stake is transmitted from cell to cell. Nevertheless we are authorized to report that a recently discovered genetic process is repeated in the Mimer and that the model 'is linked to the copy by the same relationship that links the seed to the tree'. I hope that all this has some meaning for you, and I beg you to excuse my company's reticence. You'll understand: not all the details of the apparatus are as yet covered by a patent.'

Contrary to all normal business procedures, I was unable to disguise my admiration. This was truly a revolutionary technique: organic synthesis at low temperature and pressure, order from disorder silently, rapidly, and inexpensively – the dream of four generations of chemists.

'You know, they didn't achieve this easily: as the story goes, the forty technicians assigned to Project Mimer, who had already brilliantly solved the fundamental problem, that is, the problem of oriented synthesis, for two years obtained only mirror-like copies, I mean reversed and therefore unusable. The NATCA management was already about to begin producing the device anyway, even though it would have to be activated twice for each duplication, entailing twice the expense and twice the time; then the first direct reproduction specimen was supposedly realized by chance, thanks to a providential assembling error.'

'All this leaves me perplexed,' I said. 'Every invention is usually accompanied by a story, probably bruited about by its less ingenious competitors, a story that explains the discovery by the felicitous intervention of chance.'

'Maybe,' Simpson said. 'At any rate, there is still a long way to go. You should know right from the start that the Mimer is not a rapid duplicator. For a model of approximately one hundred grams it takes no less than an hour. Furthermore there exists another limitation, obvious in itself: it cannot reproduce, or it does so only imperfectly, models that contain elements not present in the available pabulum. Other special, more complete pabula have already been realized for specific needs, but apparently they've run into difficulties with a number of elements, mainly with the heavy metals. For example (and he showed me a delightful page of an illuminated Codex), till now it is impossible to reproduce the gilding, which in fact is absent in the copy. And for all the more reason it is impossible to reproduce a coin.'

At this point I was startled once more, but this time it wasn't my chemist's viscera that reacted, but rather the coexistent and closely commingled viscera of the practical man. Not a coin, but what about a bank note? a rare stamp? or more decently and elegantly, a diamond? Does the law perhaps punish 'fabricators and vendors of fake diamonds'? Do there exist fake diamonds? Who could prevent me from putting a

101

few grams of carbon atoms into the Mimer and rearranging them in an honest tetrahedic order, and then selling the result? Nobody: not the law, and not even my conscience.

In such matters, the essential thing is to get there first, because no imagination is more industrious than that of men greedy for gain. So I set aside all hesitation, bargained moderately over the Mimer's price (which in any case was not excessive), obtained a 5 per cent discount and payment terms for a period of 120 days, and ordered the apparatus.

The Mimer, together with fifty pounds of pabulum, was delivered to me two months later. Christmas was coming; my family was in the mountains, and I had remained alone in town, devoting myself intensely to study and work. To begin with, I read the instructions several times, until I almost knew them by heart; then I took the first object at hand (it was a common gambling die) and prepared to reproduce it.

I placed it in the cell, brought the machine to the prescribed temperature, opened the small graduated valve for the pabulum and waited. There was a slight hum and from the discharge tube of the reproduction cell issued a weak gaseous spurt: it had a curious odour, similar to that of not very clean newborn babies. After an hour, I opened the cell: it contained a die exactly identical with the model in shape, colour and weight. It was lukewarm, but it soon acquired the temperature of the room. From the second die I made a third, and from the third a fourth, easily and without the slightest hitch.

I became more and more curious about the Mimer's inner mechanism, which Simpson had not been able (or not wanted?) to explain to me with satisfactory precision, and about which there was no mention in the instructions. I detached the hermetic cover of cell B, opened a small window in it with a saw, attached to it a small glass slide, sealed it firmly and put the cover back in place. Then I again introduced the die into cell A, and through the window I attentively observed what was happening in cell B during the duplication. Something extremely interesting took place: the die formed gradually, starting from below, in extremely thin superimposed layers, as though it were growing from the base of the cell. Half way through the duplication, half of the die was perfectly formed, and you could clearly distinguish the section of the wood with all of its veins. It seemed permissible to deduce that in cell A some analysing device 'explored' by lines or by planes the body to be reproduced, and transmitted to cell B the instructions for the fixing of the single particle, perhaps of the very atoms, drawn from the pabulum.

I was satisfied with the preliminary test. The next day I bought a small diamond and made a reproduction of it which proved to be perfect. From the first two diamonds I made another two; from the four another four, and so on in geometric progression until the cell of the Mimer was full. At the end of the operation, it was impossible to pick out the original diamond. In twelve hours of work I had produced $2^{12} - 1$ pieces, that is, 4,095 new diamonds; the initial investment for the equipment was amply amortized, and I felt authorized to go on to further experiments of greater or lesser interest.

The following day I duplicated without difficulty a sugar cube, a handkerchief, a railroad timetable and a pack of playing cards. The third day I tried it on a hardboiled egg: the shell turned out thin and insubstantial (for lack of calcium, I suppose), but albumen and yolk were completely normal in appearance and taste. Then I obtained a satisfactory replica of a pack of cigarettes; a box of safety matches was perfect-looking but the matches didn't light. A white and black photograph gave an extremely faded copy due to lack of silver in the pabulum. Of my wristwatch I was able to reproduce only the band, and the watch itself from then on proved useless, for reasons that I'm unable to explain.

103

The fourth day I duplicated a number of fresh beans and peas and a tulip bulb, whose germinating power I promised myself to check on. Besides these, I duplicated a quarter pound of cheese, a sausage, a round of bread and a pear, and ate it all for lunch without perceiving any difference from the respective originals. I realized that it was also possible to reproduce liquids, placing in cell B a container identical to or larger than the one containing the model in cell A.

The fifth day I went up into the attic and searched until I found a live spider. It must certainly be impossible to reproduce moving objects with precision: therefore I kept the spider in the cold on the balcony until it was numb. Then I introduced it in the Mimer; an hour later I had an impeccable replica. I marked the original with a drop of ink, put the two twins in a glass jar on the radiator, and began to wait. After half an hour the two spiders began to move simultaneously, and immediately started to fight. Their strength and skill were identical, and they fought for more than an hour without either one being able to prevail. At that I put them in two different boxes. The next day both had woven a circular web with fourteen spokes.

The sixth day I took apart the small garden wall stone by stone and found a hibernating lizard. Its double was externally normal, but when I brought it back to room temperature I noticed that it moved with great difficulty. It died within a few hours, and I was able to ascertain that its skeleton was very weak: in particular, the long bones of its small paws were flexible as rubber.

On the seventh day I rested. I phoned Mr Simpson and asked him to call on me right away; I told him about the experiments I had performed (not about the experiment with the diamonds, naturally), and, with the most insouciant facial expression and tone of voice I could muster, I asked a number of questions and made some proposals. What exactly was the Mimer's patent status? Was it possible to obtain a more complete pabulum from NATCA containing, even in small quantities, all the elements necessary for life? Was there available a larger Mimer with a five-litre capacity, able to reproduce a cat? or a two-hundred-litre capacity, able to duplicate . . .

I saw Mr Simpson turn pale. 'Good lord,' he said to me, 'I . . . I am not willing to follow you along this path. I sell automated poets, calculators, confessors, translators and duplicators. But I believe in the immortal soul, I believe I possess one and I do not wish to lose it. And neither do I wish to collaborate in creating one with the methods you have in mind. The Mimer is what it is: an ingenious machine for copying documents, and what you propose is . . . I'm sorry, but it's disgusting.'

I was not prepared for such an impetuous reaction on the part of mild Mr Simpson, and I tried to bring him to his senses: I pointed out to him that the Mimer was something, was much more than an office duplicator, and the fact that its very creators were not aware of it could mean a fortune for me and for him. I insisted on the twofold aspect of its virtues: the economical aspect as creator of order and thus of wealth, and the – how shall I put it? – Promethean aspect of a new and refined instrument for the advancement of our knowledge concerning vital mechanisms. In the end, rather obliquely, I also hinted at the experiment with the diamonds.

But it was all useless: Mr Simpson was disturbed, and he seemed incapable of understanding what I was saying. In obvious contradiction to his interest as a salesman and corporation man, he said that it was 'a bunch of nonsense', that he only believed the information printed in the presentation pamphlet, that he was not interested in adventures of thought nor tremendous profits, and that in any event he didn't want to be involved in this business. I had the impression that he

105

wished to add something else; but then he said an abrupt goodbye and left.

It is always painful to break off a friendship. I had the firm intention of getting in touch with Mr Simpson again and I was convinced that a basis for agreement, or even collaboration, could be found. I certainly meant to telephone him or write to him; yet, as unfortunately happens during periods of intense work, I put it off from one day to the next until the beginning of February, when among my mail I found a circular letter from NATCA, accompanied by a frosty note from the Milan agency signed personally by Mr Simpson: 'We hereby bring to your attention the NATCA circular, of which we attach a copy and translation.'

No one will shake my conviction that it was Mr Simpson himself, moved by his foolish moralistic scruples, who caused it to be distributed by the company. I do not repeat the entire text, too long for these notes, but the essential clause runs as follows:

The Mimer, as is true of all NATCA duplicators in existence or yet to be fabricated, is put on the market for the sole purpose of reproducing office documents. NATCA agencies are authorized to sell them only to legally constituted commercial or industrial firms, and *not to private persons*. In each case the sale of this equipment will take place only upon the purchaser's releasing a declaration in which he states and promises that he will not use the apparatus for:

the reproduction of paper money, cheques, IOUs, stamps, or other analogous objects that correspond to a definite monetary value;

the reproduction of paintings, drawings, etchings, sculptures, or other works of figurative art;

the reproduction of plants, animals, *human beings*, be

they living or defunct, or parts thereof. NATCA will not be responsible for the actions of its customers or users of its machines, which conflict with their signed declarations.

It is my opinion that these limitations will not contribute much to the Mimer's commercial success, and I will certainly point this out to Mr Simpson if, as I hope, I shall once more have the opportunity to meet with him. It is incredible how reputably reasonable people will do things that are in such obvious conflict with their own interests.

In the Christian tradition, it is God who (p. 99) created existence out of Chaos and (p. 104) rested 'on the seventh day'. Like his fellow-Italian Dino Buzzati (p. 1–8), Levi is building on European traditions such as the legends of Midas or Doctor Faustus. Or of Prometheus (p. 105), who passed to human beings the gods' knowledge of how to use fire, for which he was savagely punished.

Pabulum (p. 100 and after) is normally nutriment for a living thing. Here, as 'fuel' for the Mimer, it is a mysterious blend, 'kept under wraps'. It smells of 'not very clean newborn babies' (p. 102) and is thought to be made up (as human beings are) 'of not very stable composites of carbon and of other principal vital elements' (p. 100) – but not of metals, which it cannot reproduce. The tale may seem light at first; but the implications here point back to Auschwitz.

Levi is appalled at the responsibility of scientists and at how they may betray it. A sequel story to 'Order on the Cheap' describes a character called Gilberto as 'a symbol of our century . . . he would build an atom bomb and drop it on Milan "to see the effect it would have."' (Actually Gilberto uses the

Mimer to duplicate his wife!) *In the present story, the narrator's only anxiety is (p. 103) whether 'the initial investment' is 'amply amortized' (a dry technical – pseudo-scientific? – term for the paying off of a debt or expenses).*

The first-person viewpoint tries to seduce us into agreeing that nothing matters except self-interest: for example in the final sentence. Do you identify as much with this narrator as with that of 'The Bewitched Jacket'? Or does his obsessive self-engrossment, or his boffin's style, keep you at a distance, as I suggested might be the effect of the quite different style of 'A Telephone Call'?

FOR FURTHER READING:

The Sixth Day – the volume of science-fiction fables from which this story is taken. Or, when you're feeling strong, Levi's accounts of Auschwitz: *If This is a Man* and *The Truce*. (Michael Joseph and Abacus).

DONALD BARTHELME

★

Donald Barthelme (1931–89) was born in Texas and lived for most of his life in New York. His 'disruptive' fiction – mainly short stories, surreal, scornful, and sick-humorous – is particularly characteristic of the 1960s and early 70s. A similar anarchic imagination – though softened up for popular consumption – became familiar to TV audiences in the British series *Monty Python's Flying Circus*.

Some of Us Had Been Threatening Our Friend Colby

———————————— ★ ————————————

Some of us had been threatening our friend Colby for a long time, because of the way he had been behaving. And now he'd gone too far, so we decided to hang him. Colby argued that just because he had gone too far (he did not deny that he had gone too far) did not mean that he should be subjected to hanging. Going too far, he said, was something everybody did sometimes. We didn't pay much attention to this argument. We asked him what sort of music he would like played at the hanging. He said he'd think about it but it would take him a while to decide. I pointed out that we'd have to know soon, because Howard, who is a conductor, would have to hire and rehearse the musicians and he couldn't begin until he knew what the music was going to be. Colby said he'd always been fond of Ives's Fourth Symphony. Howard said that this was a 'delaying tactic' and that everybody knew that the Ives was almost impossible to perform and would involve weeks of rehearsal, and that the size of the orchestra and chorus would put us way over the music budget. 'Be reasonable,' he said to Colby. Colby said he'd try to think of something a little less exacting.

Hugh was worried about the wording of the invitations. What if one of them fell into the hands of the authorities? Hanging Colby was doubtless against the law, and if the authorities learned in advance what the plan was they would very likely come in and try to mess everything up. I said that although hanging Colby was almost certainly against the law, we had a perfect *moral* right to do so because he was *our* friend, *belonged* to us in various important senses, and he had after all gone too far. We agreed that the invitations would be worded in such a way that the person invited could not know for sure what he was being invited to. We decided to refer to the event as 'An Event Involving Mr Colby Williams'. A handsome script was selected from a catalogue and we picked a cream-coloured paper. Magnus said he'd see to having the invitations printed, and wondered whether we should serve drinks. Colby said he thought drinks would be nice but was worried about the expense. We told him kindly that the expense didn't matter, that we were after all his dear friends and if a group of his dear friends couldn't get together and do the thing with a little bit of *éclat*, why, what was the world coming to? Colby asked if he would be able to have drinks, too, before the event. We said, 'Certainly.'

The next item of business was the gibbet. None of us knew too much about gibbet design, but Tomás, who is an architect, said he'd look it up in old books and draw the plans. The important thing, as far as he recollected, was that the trapdoor function perfectly. He said that just roughly, counting labour

110

and materials, it shouldn't run us more than four hundred dollars. 'Good God!' Howard said. He said what was Tomás figuring on, rosewood? No, just a good grade of pine, Tomás said. Victor asked if unpainted pine wouldn't look kind of 'raw', and Tomás replied that he thought it could be stained a dark walnut without too much trouble.

I said that although I thought the whole thing ought to be done really well and all, I also thought four hundred dollars for a gibbet, on top of the expense for the drinks, invitations, musicians, and everything, was a bit steep, and why didn't we just use a tree – a nice-looking oak, or something? I pointed out that since it was going to be a June hanging the trees would be in glorious leaf and that not only would a tree add a kind of 'natural' feeling but it was also strictly traditional, especially in the West. Tomás, who had been sketching gibbets on the backs of envelopes, reminded us that an outdoor hanging always had to contend with the threat of rain. Victor said he liked the idea of doing it outdoors, possibly on the bank of a river, but noted that we would have to hold it some distance from the city, which presented the problem of getting the guests, musicians, etc., to the site and then back to town.

At this point everybody looked at Harry, who runs a car-and-truck-rental business. Harry said he thought he could round up enough limousines to take care of that end but that the drivers would have to be paid. The drivers, he pointed out, wouldn't be friends of Colby's and couldn't be expected to donate their services, any more than the bartender or the musicians. He said that he had about ten limousines, which he used mostly for funerals, and that he could probably obtain another dozen by calling around to friends of his in the trade. He said also that if we did it outside, in the open air, we'd better figure on a tent or awning of some kind to cover at least the principals and the orchestra, because if the hanging was being rained on he thought it would look kind

111

of dismal. As between gibbet and tree, he said, he had no particular preferences and he really thought that the choice ought to be left up to Colby, since it was his hanging. Colby said that everybody went too far, sometimes, and weren't we being a little Draconian? Howard said rather sharply that all that had already been discussed, and which did he want, gibbet or tree? Colby asked if he could have a firing squad. No, Howard said, he could not. Howard said a firing squad would just be an ego trip for Colby, the blindfold and last-cigarette bit, and that Colby was in enough hot water already without trying to 'upstage' everyone with unnecessary theatrics. Colby said he was sorry, he hadn't meant it that way, he'd take the tree. Tomás crumpled up the gibbet sketches he'd been making, in disgust.

Then the question of the hangman came up. Pete said did we really need a hangman? Because if we used a tree, the noose could be adjusted to the appropriate level and Colby could just jump off something – a chair or stool or something. Besides, Pete said, he very much doubted if there were any freelance hangmen wandering around the country, now that capital punishment has been done away with absolutely, temporarily, and that we'd probably have to fly one in from England or Spain or one of the South American countries, and even if we did that how could we know in advance that the man was a professional, a real hangman, and not just some money-hungry amateur who might bungle the job and shame us all, in front of everybody? We all agreed then that Colby should just jump off something and that a chair was not what he should jump off, because that would look, we felt, extremely tacky – some old kitchen chair sitting out there under our beautiful tree. Tomás, who is quite modern in outlook and not afraid of innovation, proposed that Colby be standing on a large round rubber ball ten feet in diameter. This, he said, would afford a sufficient 'drop' and would also roll out of the way if Colby suddenly changed his mind after jumping off. He reminded us that by not using a regular hangman we were placing an awful lot of the responsibility for the success of the affair on Colby himself, and that although he was sure Colby would perform creditably and not disgrace his friends at the last minute, still, men have been known to get a little irresolute at times like that, and the ten-foot-round rubber ball, which could probably be fabricated rather cheaply, would insure a 'bang-up' production right down to the wire.

At the mention of 'wire', Hank, who had been silent all this time, suddenly spoke up and said he wondered if it wouldn't be better if we used wire instead of rope – more efficient and in the end kinder to Colby, he suggested. Colby began looking a little green, and I didn't blame him, because there is something extremely distasteful in thinking about being hanged with wire instead of rope– it gives you a sort of a revulsion, when you think about it. I thought it was really quite unpleasant of Hank to be sitting there talking about wire, just when we had solved the problem of what Colby was going to jump off of so neatly, with Tomás's idea about the rubber ball, so I hastily said that wire was out of the question, because it would injure the tree – cut into the branch it was tied to when Colby's full weight hit it – and that in these days of increased respect for the environment, we didn't want that, did we? Colby gave me a grateful look, and the meeting broke up.

Everything went off very smoothly on the day of the event (the music Colby finally picked was standard stuff, Elgar, and it was played very well by Howard and his boys). It didn't rain, the event was well attended, and we didn't run out of Scotch, or anything. The ten-foot rubber ball had been painted a deep green and blended in well with the bucolic setting. The two things I remember best about the whole episode are the grateful look Colby gave me when I said what I said about the wire, and the fact that nobody has ever gone too far again.

DONALD BARTHELME

★

The plot is theoretically possible, but socially so offensive as to be ludicrous. If you don't find the story merely a very bad joke, then the key to its comic success is its tone. On p. 110 Howard complains to Colby: 'Be reasonable.' But hanging Colby is not reasonable; and what makes it even more unreasonable is the reasonableness with which it is treated, both in the committee discussions and in the deadpan narrative style.

The tone never falters: the writer keeps his nerve, and indeed twists the screw a little further in each paragraph ('Then the question of . . .' 'At the mention of . . .'). The same is true of the details of setting or properties which conventionally bring a story to life: the 'cream-coloured paper', the image of 'some old kitchen chair sitting out there under our beautiful tree' and the ten-foot rubber ball which takes its place, 'painted a deep green' to blend in 'with the bucolic setting' – these are things which (part of us howls) should never have been brought to life; to create them is anarchic.

If you like this, try moving on to the man who did it first and best, the eighteenth-century political satirist Jonathan Swift.

FOR FURTHER READING:

Forty Stories by Donald Barthelme (Secker & Warburg). *A Modest Proposal* by Jonathan Swift is an outraged protest-piece which ironically proposes to serve up pauper children as tasty dishes, since that would be no more inhumane than the way they are currently treated. *Gulliver's Travels*, Swift's full-length novel, is world-famous as grotesque fantasy but is primarily a savage political satire. (Penguin and other editions).

PETER CAREY

★

Peter Carey has an international reputation for his novels
and stories. He was born in Australia and now lives in New
York. This story is autobiographical.

A Letter to Our Son

───────────────── ★ ─────────────────

Before I have finished writing this, the story of how you were
born, I will be forty-four years old and the events and
feelings which make up the story will be at least eight months
old. You are lying in the next room in a cotton jumpsuit.
You have five teeth. You cannot walk. You do not seem
interested in crawling. You are sound asleep.

I have put off writing this so long that, now the time is
here, I do not want to write it. I cannot think. Laziness.
Wooden shutters over the memory. Nothing comes, no pictures, no feelings, but the architecture of the hospital at Camperdown.

You were born in the King George V Hospital in Missenden Road, Camperdown, a building that won an award
for its architecture. It was opened during the Second World
War, but its post-Bauhaus modern style has its roots in that
time before the First World War, with an optimism about the
technological future that we may never have again.

I liked this building. I liked its smooth, rounded, shiny

corners. I liked its wide stairs. I liked the huge sash windows, even the big blue and white checked tiles: when I remember this building there is sunshine splashed across those tiles, but there were times when it seemed that other memories might triumph and it would be remembered for the harshness of its neon lights and emptiness of the corridors.

A week before you were born, I sat with your mother in a four-bed ward on the eleventh floor of this building. In this ward she received blood transfusions from plum-red plastic bags suspended on rickety stainless steel stands. The blood did not always flow smoothly. The bags had to be fiddled with, the stand had to be raised, lowered, have its drip-rate increased, decreased, inspected by the sister who had been a political prisoner in Chile, by the sister from the Solomon Islands, by others I don't remember. The blood entered your mother through a needle in her forearm. When the vein collapsed, a new one had to be found. This was caused by a kind of bruising called 'tissuing'. We soon knew all about tissuing. It made her arm hurt like hell.

She was bright-eyed and animated as always, but her lips had a slight blue tinge and her skin had a tight, translucent quality.

She was in this room on the west because her blood appeared to be dying. Some thought the blood was killing itself. This is what we all feared, none more than me, for when I heard her blood-count was so low, the first thing I thought (stop that thought, cut it off, bury it) was cancer.

This did not necessarily have a lot to do with Alison, but with me, and how I had grown up, with a mother who was preoccupied with cancer and who, going into surgery for suspected breast cancer, begged the doctor to 'cut them both off'. When my mother's friend Enid Tanner boasted of her hard stomach muscles, my mother envisaged a growth. When her father complained of a sore elbow, my mother threatened the old man: 'All right, we'll take you up to Doctor Campbell and she'll cut it off.' When I was ten, my mother's brother got cancer and they cut his leg off right up near the hip and took photographs of him, naked one-legged, to show other doctors the success of the operation.

When I heard your mother's blood-count was low, I was my mother's son. I thought: cancer.

I remembered what Alison had told me of that great tragedy of her grandparents' life, how their son (her uncle) had leukaemia, how her grandfather then bought him the car (a Ford Prefect? a Morris Minor?) he had hitherto refused him, how the dying boy had driven for miles and miles, hours and hours while his cells attacked each other.

I tried to stop this thought, to cut it off. It grew again, like a thistle whose root has not been removed and must grow again, every time, stronger and stronger.

The best haematological unit in Australia was on hand to deal with the problem. They worked in the hospital across the road, the Royal Prince Alfred. They were friendly and efficient. They were not at all like I had imagined big hospital specialists to be. They took blood samples, but the blood did not tell them enough. They returned to take marrow from your mother's bones. They brought a big needle with them that would give you the horrors if you could see the size of it.

The doctor's speciality was leukaemia, but he said to us: 'We don't think it's anything really nasty.' Thus 'nasty' became a code for cancer.

They diagnosed megnoblastic anaemia which, although we did not realize it, is the condition of the blood and not the disease itself.

Walking back through the streets in Shimbashi in Tokyo, your mother once told me that a fortune-teller had told her she would die young. It was for this reason – or so I remembered – that she took such care of her health. At the

117

time she told me this, we had not known each other very long. It was July. We had fallen in love in May. We were still stumbling over each other's feelings in the dark. I took this secret of your mother's lightly, not thinking about the weight it must carry, what it might mean to talk about it. I hurt her; we fought, in the street by the Shimbashi railway station, in a street with shop windows advertising cosmetic surgery, in the Dai-Ichi Hotel in the Ginza district of Tokyo, Japan.

When they took the bone marrow from your mother's spine, I held her hand. The needle had a cruel diameter, was less a needle than an instrument for removing a plug. She was very brave. Her wrists seemed too thin, her skin too white and shiny, her eyes too big and bright. She held my hand because of pain. I held hers because I loved her, because I could not think of living if I did not have her. I thought of what she had told me in Tokyo. I wished there was a God I could pray to.

I flew to Canberra on 7 May 1984. It was my forty-first birthday. I had injured my back and should have been lying flat on a board. I had come from a life with a woman which had reached, for both of us, a state of chronic unhappiness. I will tell you the truth: I was on that aeroplane to Canberra because I hoped I might fall in love. This made me a dangerous person.

There was a playwrights' conference in Canberra. I hoped there would be a woman there who would love me as I would love her. This was a fantasy I had had before, getting on aeroplanes to foreign cities, riding in taxis towards hotels in Melbourne, in Adelaide, in Brisbane. I do not mean that I was thinking about sex, or an affair, but that I was looking for someone to spend my life with. Also – and I swear I have not invented this after the fact – I had a vision of your mother's neck.

I hardly knew her. I met her once at a dinner when I hardly noticed her. I met her a second time when I saw, in a meeting room, the back of her neck. We spoke that time, but I was argumentative and I did not think of her in what I can only call 'that way'.

And yet as the aeroplane came down to land in Canberra, I saw your mother's neck, and thought: maybe Alison Summers will be there. She was the dramaturge at the Nimrod Theatre. It was a playwrights' conference. She should be there.

And she was. And we fell in love. And we stayed up till four in the morning every morning talking. And there were other men, everywhere, in love with her. I didn't know about the other men. I knew only that I was in love as I had not been since I was eighteen years old. I wanted to marry Alison Summers, and at the end of the first night we had been out together when I walked her to the door of her room, and we had, for the first time, ever so lightly, kissed on the lips – and also, I must tell you, for it was delectable and wonderful, I kissed your mother on her long, beautiful neck – and when we had kissed and patted the air between us and said 'all right' a number of times, and I had walked back to my room where I had, because of my back injury, a thin mattress lying flat on the floor, and when I was in this bed, I said, aloud, to the empty room: 'I am going to live with Alison.'

And I went to sleep so happy I must have been smiling.

She did not know what I told the room. And it was three or four days before I could see her again, three or four days before we could go out together, spend time alone, and I could tell her what I thought.

I had come to Canberra wanting to fall in love. Now I was in love. Who was I in love with? I hardly knew, and yet I knew exactly. I did not even realize how beautiful she was. I found that out later. At the beginning I recognized something more potent than beauty: it was a force, a life, an energy. She had such life in her face, in her eyes – those eyes which you inherited – most of all. It was this I loved, this which I recognized so that I could say – having kissed her so lightly – I will live with Alison. And I know that I was right.

It was a conference. We were behaving like men and women do at conferences, having affairs. We would not be so sleazy. After four nights staying up talking till four a.m. we had still not made love. I would creep back to my room, to my mattress on the floor. We talked about everything. Your mother liked me, but I cannot tell you how long it took her to fall in love with me. But I know we were discussing marriages and babies when we had not even been to bed together. That came early one morning when I returned to her room after three hours' sleep. We had not planned to make love there at the conference but there we were, lying on the bed, kissing, and then we were making love, and you were not conceived then, of course, and yet from that time we never ceased thinking of you and when, later in Sydney, we had to learn to adjust to each other's needs, and when we argued, which we did often then, it was you more than anything that kept us together. We wanted you so badly. We loved you before we saw you. We loved you as we made you, in bed in another room, at Lovett Bay.

When your mother came to the eleventh floor of the King George V Hospital, you were almost ready to be born. Every day the sisters came and smeared jelly on your mother's tight, bulging stomach and then stuck a flat little octopus-type sucker to it and listened to the noises you made.

You sounded like soldiers marching on a bridge.

You sounded like short-wave radio.

You sounded like the inside of the sea.

We did not know if you were a boy or a girl, but we called

you Sam anyway. When you kicked or turned we said: 'Sam's doing his exercises.' We said silly things.

When we heard how low Alison's blood-count was, I phoned the obstetrician to see if you were OK. She said there was no need to worry. She said you had your own blood supply. She said that as long as the mother's count was above six there was no need to worry.

Your mother's count was 6.2. This was very close. I kept worrying that you had been hurt in some way. I could not share this worry for to share it would only be to make it worse. Also I recognize that I have made a whole career out of making my anxieties get up and walk around, not only in my own mind, but in the minds of readers. I went to see a naturopath once. We talked about negative emotions – fear and anger. I said to him: 'But I *use* my anger and my fear.' I talked about these emotions as if they were chisels and hammers.

This alarmed him considerably.

Your mother is not like this. When the haematologists saw how she looked, they said: 'Our feeling is that you don't have anything nasty.' They topped her up with blood until her count was twelve and although they had not located the source of her anaemia, they sent her home.

A few days later her count was down to just over six.

It seemed as if there was a silent civil war inside her veins and arteries. The number of casualties was appalling.

I think we both got frightened then. I remember coming home to Louisa Road. I remember worrying that I would cry. I remember embracing your mother – and you too, for you were a great bulge between us. I must not cry. I must support her.

I made a meal. It was a salade niçoise. The electric lights, in memory, were all ten watts, sapped by misery. I could barely eat. I think we may have watched a funny film on videotape. We repacked the bag that had been unpacked so short a time before. It now seemed likely that your birth was to be induced. If your mother was sick she could not be looked after properly with you inside her. She would be given one more blood transfusion, and then the induction would begin. And that is how your birthday would be on September thirteenth.

Two nights before your birthday I sat with Alison in the four-bed ward, the one facing east, towards Missenden Road. The curtains were drawn around us. I sat on the bed and held her hand. The blood continued its slow viscous drip from the plum-red bag along the clear plastic tube and into her arm. The obstetrician was with us. She stood at the head of the bed, a kind, intelligent woman in her early thirties. We talked about Alison's blood. We asked her what she thought this mystery could be. Really what we wanted was to be told that everything was OK. There was a look on Alison's face when she asked. I cannot describe it, but it was not a face seeking medical 'facts'.

The obstetrician went through all the things that were not wrong with your mother's blood. She did not have a vitamin B deficiency. She did not have a folic acid deficiency. There was no iron deficiency. She did not have any of the common (and easily fixable) anaemias of pregnancy. So what could it be? we asked, really only wishing to be assured it was nothing 'nasty'.

'Well,' said the obstetrician, 'at this stage you cannot rule out cancer.'

I watched your mother's face. Nothing in her expression showed what she must feel. There was a slight colouring of her cheeks. She nodded. She asked a question or two. She held my hand, but there was no tight squeezing.

The obstetrician asked Alison if she was going to be 'all right.' Alison said she would be 'all right'. But when the obstetrician left she left the curtains drawn.

The obstetrician's statement was not of course categorical and not everyone who has cancer dies, but Alison was, at that instant, confronting the thing that we fear most. When the doctor said those words, it was like a dream or a nightmare. I heard them said. And yet they were not said. They could not be said. And when we hugged each other – when the doctor had gone – we pressed our bodies together as we always had before, and if there were tears on our cheeks, there had been tears on our cheeks before. I kissed your mother's eyes. Her hair was wet with her tears. I smoothed her hair on her forehead. My own eyes were swimming. She said: 'All right, how are we going to get through all this?'

Now you know her, you know how much like her that is. She is not going to be a victim of anything.

'We'll decide it's going to be OK,' she said, 'that's all.'

And we dried our eyes.

But that night, when she was alone in her bed, waiting for the sleeping pill to work, she thought: if I die, I'll at least have made this little baby.

When I left your mother I appeared dry-eyed and positive, but my disguise was a frail shell of a thing and it cracked on the stairs and my grief and rage came spilling out in gulps. The halls of the hospital gleamed with polish and vinyl and fluorescent light. The flower-seller on the ground floor had locked up his shop. The foyer was empty. The whisker-shadowed man in admissions was watching television. In Missenden Road two boys in jeans and sand-shoes conducted separate conversations in separate phone booths. Death was not touching them. They turned their backs to each other.

One of them – a red-head with a tattoo on his forearm – laughed.

In Missenden Road there were taxis NOT FOR HIRE speeding towards other destinations.

In Missenden Road the bright white lights above the zebra crossings became a luminous sea inside my eyes. Car lights turned into necklaces and ribbons. I was crying, thinking it is not for me to cry: crying is a poison, a negative force; everything will be all right; but I was weeping as if huge balloons of air had to be released from inside my guts. I walked normally. My grief was invisible. A man rushed past me, carrying roses wrapped in cellophane. I got into my car. The floor was littered with car-park tickets from all the previous days of blood transfusions, tests, test results, admission etc. I drove out of the car park. I talked aloud.

I told the night I loved Alison Summers. I love you, I love you, you will not die. There were red lights at the Parramatta Road. I sat there, howling, unroadworthy. I love you.

The day after tomorrow there will be a baby. Will the baby have a mother? What would we do if we knew Alison was dying? What would we do so Sam would know his mother? Would we make a videotape? Would we hire a camera? Would we set it up and act for you? Would we talk to you with smiling faces, showing you how we were together, how we loved each other? How could we? How could we think of these things?

I was a prisoner in a nightmare driving down Ross Street in Glebe. I passed the Afrikan restaurant where your mother and I ate after first coming to live in Balmain.

All my life I have waited for this woman. This cannot happen.

I thought: Why would it *not* happen? Every day people are tortured, killed, bombed. Every day babies starve. Every day there is pain and grief, enough to make you howl to the moon forever. Why should we be exempt, I thought, from the pain of life?

What would I do with a baby? How would I look after it? Day after day, minute after minute, by myself. I would be a sad man, forever, marked by the loss of this woman. I would love the baby. I would care for it. I would see, in its features, every day, the face of the woman I had loved more than any other.

When I think of this time, it seems as if it's two in the morning, but it was not. It was ten o'clock at night. I drove home through a landscape of grotesque imaginings.

The house was empty and echoing.

In the nursery everything was waiting for you, all the things we had got for 'the baby'. We had read so many books about babies, been to classes where we learned about how babies are born, but we still did not understand the purpose of all the little clothes we had folded in the drawers. We did not know which was a swaddle and which was a sheet. We could not have selected the clothes to dress you in.

I drank coffee. I drank wine. I set out to telephone Kathy Lette, Alison's best friend, so she would have this 'news' before she spoke to your mother the next day. I say 'set out' because each time I began to dial, I thought: I am not going to do this properly. I hung up. I did deep breathing. I calmed myself. I telephoned. Kim Williams, Kathy's husband, answered and said Kathy was not home yet. I thought: she must know. I told Kim, and as I told him the weeping came with it. I could hear myself. I could imagine Kim listening to me. I would sound frightening, grotesque, and less in control than I was. When I had finished frightening him, I went to bed and slept.

I do not remember the next day, only that we were bright and determined. Kathy hugged Alison and wept. I hugged Kathy and wept. There were isolated incidents. We were 'handling it'. And, besides, you were coming on the next day. You were life, getting stronger and stronger.

I had practical things to worry about. For instance: the bag. The bag was to hold all the things for the labour ward. There was a list for the contents of the bag and these contents were all purchased and ready, but still I must bring them to the hospital early the next morning. I checked the bag. I placed things where I would not forget them. You wouldn't believe the things we had. We had a cassette-player and a tape with soothing music. We had rosemary and lavender oil so I could massage your mother and relax her between contractions. I had a thermos to fill with blocks of frozen orange juice. There were special cold packs to relieve the pain of a backache labour. There were paper pants – your arrival, after all, was not to happen without a great deal of mess. There were socks, because your mother's feet would almost certainly get very cold. I packed all these things, and there was something in the process of this packing which helped overcome my fears and made me concentrate on you, our little baby, already so loved although we did not know your face, had seen no more of you than the ghostly blue image thrown up by the ultrasound in the midst of whose shifting perspectives we had seen your little hand move. ('He waved to us.')

On the morning of the day of your birth I woke early. It was only just light. I had notes stuck on the fridge and laid out on the table. I made coffee and poured it into a thermos. I made the bagel sandwiches your mother and I had planned months before – my lunch. I filled the bagels with a fiery Polish sausage and cheese and gherkins. For your mother, I filled a spray-bottle with Evian water.

It was a Saturday morning and bright and sunny and I

knew you would be born but I did not know what it would be like. I drove along Ross Street in Glebe ignorant of the important things I would know that night. I wore grey stretchy trousers and a black shirt which would later be marked by the white juices of your birth. I was excited, but less than you might imagine. I parked at the hospital as I had parked on all those other occasions. I carried the bags up to the eleventh floor. They were heavy.

Alison was in her bed. She looked calm and beautiful. When we kissed, her lips were soft and tender. She said: 'This time tomorrow we'll have a little baby.'

In our conversation, we used the diminutive a lot. You were always spoken of as 'little', as indeed you must really have been, but we would say 'little' hand, 'little' feet, 'little' baby, and this evoked all our powerful feelings about you.

This term ('little') is so loaded that writers are wary of using it. It is cute, sentimental, 'easy'. All of sentient life seems programmed to respond to 'little'. If you watch grown dogs with a pup, a pup they have never seen, they are immediately patient and gentle, even solicitous, with it. If you had watched your mother and father holding up a tiny terry-towelling jumpsuit in a department store, you would have seen their faces change as they celebrated your 'littleness' while, at the same time, making fun of their own responses – they were aware of acting in a way they would have previously thought of as saccharine.

And yet we were not aware of the torrents of emotion your 'littleness' would unleash in us, and by the end of September thirteenth we would think it was nothing other than the meaning of life itself.

When I arrived at the hospital with the heavy bags of cassette-players and rosemary oil, I saw a dark-bearded, neat man in a suit sitting out by the landing. This was the hypnotherapist who had arrived to help you come into the world. He was serious, impatient, eager to start. He wanted to start in the pathology ward, but in the end he helped carry the cassette-player, thermoses, sandwiches, massage oil, sponges, paper pants, apple juice, frozen orange blocks, rolling pin, cold packs, and even water down to the labour ward where – on a stainless steel stand eight feet high – the sisters were already hanging the bag of Oxytocin which would ensure this day was your birthday.

It was a pretty room, by the taste of the time. As I write it is still that time, and I still think it pretty. All the surfaces were hospital surfaces – easy to clean – laminexes, vinyls, materials with a hard shininess, but with colours that were soft pinks and blues and an effect that was unexpectedly pleasant, even sophisticated.

The bed was one of those complicated stainless steel machines which seems so cold and impersonal until you realize all the clever things it can do. In the wall there were sockets with labels like OXYGEN. The cupboards were filled with paper-wrapped sterile 'objects'. There was, in short, a seriousness about the room, and when we plugged in the cassette-player we took care to make sure we were not using a socket that might be required for something more important.

The hypnotherapist left me to handle the unpacking of the bags. He explained his business to the obstetrician. She told him that eight hours would be a good, fast labour. The hypnotherapist said he and Alison were aiming for three. I don't know what the doctor thought, but I thought there was not a hope in hell.

When the Oxytocin drip had been put into my darling's arm, when the water-clear hormone was entering her veins, one drip every ten seconds (you could hear the machine click when a drip was released), when these pure chemical messages were being delivered to her body, the hypnotherapist attempted to send other messages of a less easily assayable quality.

I tell you the truth: I did not care for this hypnotherapist, this pushy, over-eager fellow taking up all this room in the labour ward. He sat on the right-hand side of the bed. I sat on the left. He made me feel useless. He said: 'You are going to have a good labour, a fast labour, a fast labour like the one you have already visualized.' Your mother's eyes were closed. She had such large, soft lids, such tender and vulnerable coverings of skin. Inside the pink light of the womb, your eyelids were the same. Did you hear the messages your mother was sending to her body and to you? The hypnotherapist said: 'After just three hours you are going to deliver a baby, a good, strong, healthy baby. It will be an easy birth, an effortless birth. It will last three hours and you will not tear.' On the door the sisters had tacked a sign reading: QUIET PLEASE. HYPNOTHERAPY IN PROGRESS. 'You are going to be so relaxed, and in a moment you are going to be even more relaxed, more relaxed than you have ever been before. You are feeling yourself going deeper and deeper and when you come to you will be in a state of waking hypnosis and you will respond to the trigger-words Peter will give you during your labour, words which will make you, once again, so relaxed.'

My trigger-words were to be 'Breathe' and 'Relax'.

The hypnotherapist gave me his phone number and asked me to call when you were born. But for the moment you had not felt the effects of the Oxytocin on your world and you could not yet have suspected the adventures the day would have in store for you.

You still sounded like the ocean, like soldiers marching across a bridge, like short-wave radio.

On Tuesday nights through the previous winter we had gone

to classes in a building where the lifts were always sticking. We had walked up the stairs to a room where pregnant women and their partners had rehearsed birth with dolls, had watched hours of videotapes of exhausted women in labour. We had practised all the different sorts of breathing. We had learned of the different positions for giving birth: the squat, the supported squat, the squat supported by a seated partner. We knew the positions for first and second stage, for a backache labour, and so on, and so on. We learned birth was a complicated, exhausting and difficult process. We worried we would forget how to breathe. And yet now the time was here we both felt confident, even though nothing would be like it had been in the birth classes. Your mother was connected to the Oxytocin drip which meant she could not get up and walk around. It meant it was difficult for her to 'belly dance' or do most of the things we had spent so many evenings learning about.

In the classes they tell you that the contractions will start far apart, that you should go to hospital only when they are ten minutes apart: short bursts of pain, but long rests in between. During this period your mother could expect to walk around, to listen to music, to enjoy a massage. However, your birth was not to be like this. This was not because of you. It was because of the Oxytocin. It had a fast, intense effect, like a double Scotch when you're expecting a beer. There were not to be any ten-minute rests, and from the time the labour started it was, almost immediately, fast and furious, with a one-minute contraction followed by no more than two minutes of rest.

If there had been time to be frightened, I think I would have been frightened. Your mother was in the grip of pains she could not escape from. She squatted on a bean bag. It was as if her insides were all tangled, and tugged in a battle to the death. Blood ran from her. Fluid like egg-white. I did not know what anything was. I was a man who had wandered on to a battlefield. The blood was bright with oxygen. I wiped your mother's brow. She panted. *Huh-huh-huh-huh*. I ministered to her with sponge and water. I could not take her pain for her. I could do nothing but measure the duration of the pain. I had a little red stop-watch you will one day find abandoned in a dusty drawer. (Later your mother asked me what I had felt during labour. I thought only: I must count the seconds of the contraction; I must help Alison breathe, now, now, now; I must get that sponge – there is time to make the water in the sponge cool – now I can remove that bowl and cover it. Perhaps I can reach the bottle of Evian water. God, I'm so *thirsty*. What did I think during the labour? I thought: When this contraction is over I will get to that Evian bottle.)

Somewhere in the middle of this, in these three hours in this room whose only view was a blank screen of frosted glass, I helped your mother climb on to the bed. She was on all fours. In this position she could reach the gas mask. It was nitrous oxide, laughing gas. It did not stop the pain, but it made it less important. For the gas to work your mother had to anticipate the contraction, breathing in gas before it arrived. The sister came and showed me how I could feel the contraction coming with my hand. But I couldn't. We used the stop-watch, but the contractions were not regularly spaced, and sometimes we anticipated them and sometimes not. When we did not get it right, your mother took the full brunt of the pain. She had her face close to the mattress. I sat on the chair beside. My face was close to hers. I held the watch where she could see it. I held her wrist. I can still see the red of her face, the wideness of her eyes as they bulged at the enormous *size* of the pains that racked her.

Sisters came and went. They had to see how wide the

cervix was. At first it was only two centimetres, not nearly enough room for you to come out. An hour later they announced it was four centimetres. It had to get to nine centimetres before we could even think of you being born. There had to be room for your head (which we had been told was big – well, we were told wrong, weren't we?) and your shoulders to slip through. It felt to your mother that this labour would go on for eight or twelve or twenty hours. That she should endure this intensity of pain for this time was unthinkable. It was like running a hundred-metre race which was stretching to ten miles. She wanted an epidural – a pain blocker.

But when the sister heard this she said: 'Oh do try to hang on. You're doing *so* well.'

I went to the sister, like a shop steward.

I said: 'My wife wants an epidural, so can you please arrange it?'

The sister agreed to fetch the anaesthetist, but there was between us – I admit it now – a silent conspiracy: for although I had pressed the point and she had agreed it was your mother's right, we both believed (I, for my part, on her advice) that if your mother could endure a little longer she could have the birth she wanted – without an epidural.

The anaesthetist came and went. The pain was at its worst. A midwife came and inspected your mother. She said: 'Ten centimetres.'

She said: 'Your baby is about to be born.'

We kissed, your mother and I. We kissed with soft, passionate lips as we did the day we lay on a bed at Lovett Bay and conceived you. That day the grass outside the window was a brilliant green beneath the vibrant petals of fallen jacaranda.

Outside the penumbra of our consciousness trolleys were wheeled. Sterile bags were cut open. The contractions did not stop, of course.

The obstetrician had not arrived. She was in a car, driving fast towards the hospital.

I heard a midwife say: 'Who can deliver in this position?' (It was still unusual, as I learned at that instant, for women to deliver their babies on all fours.)

Someone left the room. Someone entered. Your mother was pressing the gas mask so hard against her face it was making deep indentations on her skin. Her eyes bulged huge.

Someone said: 'Well get her, otherwise I'll have to deliver it myself.'

The door opened. Bushfire came in.

Bushfire was aboriginal. She was about fifty years old. She was compact and tactiturn like a farmer. She had a face that folded in on itself and let out its feelings slowly, selectively. It was a face to trust, and trust especially at this moment when I looked up to see Bushfire coming through the door in a green gown. She came in a rush, her hands out to have gloves put on.

There was another contraction. I heard the latex snap around Bushfire's wrists. She said: 'There it is. I can see your baby's head.' It was you. The tip of you, the top of you. You were a new country, a planet, a star seen for the first time. I was looking at Bushfire. I was looking at your mother. She was all alight with love and pain.

'Push,' said Bushfire.

Your mother pushed. It was you she was pushing, you that put that look of luminous love on her face, you that made the veins on her forehead bulge and her skin go red.

Then – it seems such a short time later – Bushfire said: 'Your baby's head is born.'

And then, so quickly in retrospect, but one can no more recall it accurately than one can recall exactly how one made love on a bed when the jacaranda petals were lying like jewels on the grass outside. Soon. Soon we heard you. Soon you slipped out of your mother. Soon you came slithering out not having hurt her, not even having grazed her. You slipped out, as slippery as a little fish, and we heard you cry. Your cry was so much lighter and thinner than I might have expected. I do not mean that it was weak or frail, but that your first cry had a timbre unlike anything I had expected. The joy we felt. Your mother and I kissed again, at that moment.

'My little baby,' she said. We were crying with happiness. 'My little baby.'

I turned to look. I saw you. Skin. Blue-white, shiny-wet.

I said: 'It's a boy.'

'Look at me,' your mother said, meaning: stay with me, be with me, the pain is not over yet, do not leave me now. I turned to her. I kissed her. I was crying, just crying with happiness that you were there.

The room you were born in was quiet, not full of noise and clattering. This is how we wanted it for you. So you could come into the world gently and that you should – as you were now – be put on to your mother's stomach. They wrapped you up. I said: 'Couldn't he feel his mother's skin?' They unwrapped you so you could have your skin against hers.

And there you were. It was you. You had a face, the face we had never known. You were so calm. You did not cry or fret. You had big eyes like your mother's. And yet when I looked at you first I saw not your mother and me, but your two grandfathers, your mother's father, my father; and, as my father, whom I loved a great deal, had died the year before, I was moved to see that here, in you, he was alive.

Look at the photographs in the album that we took at this time. Look at your mother and how alive she is, how clear her eyes are, how all the red pain has just slipped off her face and left the unmistakable visage of a young woman in love.

We bathed you (I don't know whether this was before or

after) in warm water and you accepted this gravely, swimming instinctively.

I held you (I think this must be before), and you were warm and slippery. You had not been bathed when I held you. The obstetrician gave you to me so she could examine your mother. She said: 'Here.'

I held you against me. I knew then that your mother would not die. I thought: 'It's fine, it's all right.' I held you against my breast. You smelled of love-making.

That word 'gravely', a few lines from the end, sums up the style and tone of this narrative – an unfaltering patient seriousness (sometimes called by the Latin word gravitas*). Not only is the father setting down very important events, but he really is writing for the son to read, how many years into the future – twelve? fifteen? (How young would you have been ready to read this?) 'It was a pretty room, by the taste of the time. As I write it is still that time . . .'*

The combination of this style with this particular plot (a true story about the creation of life itself) makes us hold our breath. Above all we are touched by the distinctive viewpoint. We're used to first-person narration, nothing new about that; but this is not, apparently, being told to us: instead, we are reading someone else's most intimate letter. And yet in fact it is being shared with us; and the task of shaping it as art, for us to read, may even have made it possible to write. That task is tackled gravely: with the eye all the time on the ball – note the determination to get the details right, and neither to exaggerate nor diminish the emotions. ('I was excited, but less than you might imagine' . . . 'nothing other than the meaning of life itself.')

To set down an experience with this gravitas *takes ex-*

ceptional concentration (*eye on the ball*), motivated by a determination to tell the truth rather than go for flashy or comforting effects. Whatever our own literary ability, it's a good thing for us to try to do.

FOR FURTHER READING:

Also by Peter Carey: *The Fat Man in History* (stories); *Illywhacker*, *Oscar and Lucinda* and *The Tax Inspector* (novels). Not easy. All published by Faber.

FLANNERY O'CONNOR

Flannery O'Connor (1925–64) spent almost all her life in rural Georgia, in the southern USA. At the age of twenty-seven she learned that she was dying from the disease lupus; she lived a further twelve years on the family dairy farm, writing novels and a large number of often violent and/or comic short stories.

She was a committed Roman Catholic, in an area very largely Protestant; and white in a region with a large black population. In the early 1960s, when this story was written, buses had just been 'integrated' (blacks being allowed to sit with whites).

Everything That Rises Must Converge

Her doctor had told Julian's mother that she must lose twenty pounds on account of her blood pressure, so on Wednesday nights Julian had to take her downtown on the bus for a reducing class at the Y. The reducing class was designed for working girls over fifty, who weighed from 165 to 200 pounds. His mother was one of the slimmer ones, but she said ladies did not tell their age or weight. She would not ride the buses by herself at night since they had been integrated, and because the reducing class was one of her few pleasures, necessary for her health, and *free*, she said Julian could at least put himself out to take her, considering all she did for him. Julian did not like to consider all she did for him, but every Wednesday night he braced himself and took her.

She was almost ready to go, standing before the hall mirror, putting on her hat, while he, his hands behind him, appeared pinned to the door frame, waiting like Saint Sebastian for the arrows to begin piercing him. The hat was new and had cost her seven dollars and a half. She kept saying, 'Maybe I shouldn't have paid that for it. No, I shouldn't have. I'll take it off and return it tomorrow. I shouldn't have bought it.'

Julian raised his eyes to heaven. 'Yes, you should have bought it,' he said. 'Put it on and let's go.' It was a hideous hat. A purple velvet flap came down on one side of it and stood up on the other; the rest of it was green and looked like a cushion with the stuffing out. He decided it was less comical than jaunty and pathetic. Everything that gave her pleasure was small and depressed him.

She lifted the hat one more time and set it down slowly on top of her head. Two wings of grey hair protruded on either side of her florid face, but her eyes, sky blue, were as innocent and untouched by experience as they must have been when she was ten. Were it not that she was a widow who had struggled fiercely to feed and clothe and put him through school and who was supporting him still, 'until he got on his feet', she might have been a little girl that he had to take to town.

'It's all right, it's all right,' he said. 'Let's go.' He opened the door himself and started down the walk to get her going. The sky was a dying violet and the houses stood out darkly against it, bulbous liver-coloured monstrosities of a uniform ugliness though no two were alike. Since this had been a fashionable neighbourhood forty years ago, his mother persisted in thinking they did well to have an apartment in it. Each house had a narrow collar of dirt around it in which sat, usually, a grubby child. Julian walked with his hands in his pockets, his head down and thrust forward and his eyes glazed with the determination to make himself completely numb during the time he would be sacrificed to her pleasure.

The door closed and he turned to find the dumpy figure, surmounted by the atrocious hat, coming toward him. 'Well,' she said, 'you only live once and paying a little more for it, I at least won't meet myself coming and going.'

'Some day I'll start making money,' Julian said gloomily – he knew he never would – 'and you can have one of those jokes whenever you take the fit.' But first they would move. He visualized a place where the nearest neighbours would be three miles away on either side.

'I think you're doing fine,' she said, drawing on her gloves. 'You've only been out of school a year. Rome wasn't built in a day.'

She was one of the few members of the Y reducing class who arrived in hat and gloves and who had a son who had been to college. 'It takes time,' she said, 'and the world is in such a mess. This hat looked better on me than any of the others, though when she brought it out I said, "Take that thing back. I wouldn't have it on my head," and she said, "Now wait till you see it on," and when she put it on me, I said, "We-ull," and she said, "If you ask me, that hat does something for you and you do something for the hat, and besides," she said, "with that hat, you won't meet yourself coming and going."'

Julian thought he could have stood his lot better if she had been selfish, if she had been an old hag who drank and screamed at him. He walked along, saturated in depression, as if in the midst of his martyrdom he had lost his faith. Catching sight of his long, hopeless, irritated face, she stopped suddenly with a grief-stricken look, and pulled back on his arm. 'Wait on me,' she said. 'I'm going back to the house and take this thing off and tomorrow I'm going to return it. I was out of my head. I can pay the gas bill with the seven-fifty.'

He caught her arm in a vicious grip. 'You are not going to take it back,' he said. 'I like it.'

'Well,' she said, 'I don't think I ought . . . '

'Shut up and enjoy it,' he muttered, more depressed than ever.

'With the world in the mess it's in,' she said, 'it's a wonder we can enjoy anything. I tell you, the bottom rail is on the top.'

Julian sighed.

'Of course,' she said, 'if you know who you are, you can go anywhere.' She said this every time he took her to the reducing class. 'Most of them in it are not our kind of people,' she said, 'but I can be gracious to anybody. I know who I am.'

'They don't give a damn for your graciousness,' Julian said savagely. 'Knowing who you are is good for one generation only. You haven't the foggiest idea where you stand now or who you are.'

She stopped and allowed her eyes to flash at him. 'I most certainly do know who I am,' she said, 'and if you don't know who you are, I'm ashamed of you.'

'Oh hell,' Julian said.

'Your great-grandfather was a former governor of this state,' she said. 'Your grandfather was a prosperous land-owner. Your grandmother was a Godhigh.'

'Will you look around you,' he said tensely, 'and see where you are now?' and he swept his arm jerkily out to indicate the neighbourhood, which the growing darkness at least made less dingy.

'You remain what you are,' she said. 'Your great-grand-father had a plantation and two hundred slaves.'

'There are no more slaves,' he said irritably.

'They were better off when they were,' she said. He groaned to see that she was off on that topic. She rolled on to it every few days like a train on an open track. He knew every stop, every junction, every swamp along the way, and knew the exact point at which her conclusion would roll majestically into the station: 'It's ridiculous. It's simply not realistic. They should rise, yes, but on their own side of the fence.'

'Let's skip it,' Julian said.

'The ones I feel sorry for,' she said, 'are the ones that are half white. They're tragic.'

'Will you skip it?'

'Suppose we were half white. We would certainly have mixed feelings.'

'I have mixed feelings now,' he groaned.

'Well let's talk about something pleasant,' she said. 'I remember going to Grandpa's when I was a little girl. Then the house had double stairways that went up to what was really the second floor – all the cooking was done on the first. I used to like to stay down in the kitchen on account of the way the walls smelled. I would sit with my nose pressed against the plaster and take deep breaths. Actually the place belonged to the Godhighs but your grandfather Chestny paid the mortgage and saved it for them. They were in reduced circumstances,' she said, 'but reduced or not, they never forgot who they were.'

'Doubtless that decayed mansion reminded them,' Julian muttered. He never spoke of it without contempt or thought of it without longing. He had seen it once when he was a child before it had been sold. The double stairways had rotted and been torn down. Negroes were living in it. But it remained in his mind as his mother had known it. It appeared in his dreams regularly. He would stand on the wide porch, listening to the rustle of oak leaves, then wander through the

141

high-ceilinged hall into the parlour that opened on to it and gaze at the worn rugs and faded draperies. It occurred to him that it was he, not she, who could have appreciated it. He preferred its threadbare elegance to anything he could name and it was because of it that all the neighbourhoods they had lived in had been a torment to him – whereas she had hardly known the difference. She called her insensitivity 'being adjustable.'

'And I remember the old darky who was my nurse, Caroline. There was no better person in the world. I've always had a great respect for my coloured friends,' she said. 'I'd do anything in the world for them and they'd . . .'

'Will you for God's sake get off that subject?' Julian said. When he got on a bus by himself, he made it a point to sit down beside a Negro, in reparation as it were for his mother's sins.

'You're mighty touchy tonight,' she said. 'Do you feel all right?'

'Yes, I feel all right,' he said. 'Now lay off.'

She pursed her lips. 'Well, you certainly are in a vile humour,' she observed. 'I just won't speak to you at all.'

They had reached the bus stop. There was no bus in sight and Julian, his hands still jammed in his pockets and his head thrust forward, scowled down the empty street. The frustration of having to wait on the bus as well as ride on it began to creep up his neck like a hot hand. The presence of his mother was borne in upon him as she gave a pained sigh. He looked at her bleakly. She was holding herself very erect under the preposterous hat, wearing it like a banner of her imaginary dignity. There was in him an evil urge to break her spirit. He suddenly unloosened his tie and pulled it off and put it in his pocket.

She stiffened. 'Why must you look like *that* when you take me to town?' she said. 'Why must you deliberately embarrass me?'

142

'If you'll never learn where you are,' he said, 'you can at least learn where I am.'

'You look like a – thug,' she said.

'Then I must be one,' he murmured.

'I'll just go home,' she said. 'I will not bother you. If you can't do a little thing like that for me . . . '

Rolling his eyes upward, he put his tie back on. 'Restored to my class,' he muttered. He thrust his face toward her and hissed, 'True culture is in the mind, the *mind*,' he said, and tapped his head, 'the mind.'

'It's in the heart,' she said, 'and in how you do things and how you do things is because of who you *are*.'

'Nobody in the damn bus cares who you are.'

'I care who I am,' she said icily.

The lighted bus appeared on top of the next hill and as it approached, they moved out into the street to meet it. He put his hand under her elbow and hoisted her up on the creaking step. She entered with a little smile, as if she were going into a drawing room where everyone had been waiting for her. While he put in the tokens, she sat down on one of the broad front seats for three which faced the aisle. A thin woman with protruding teeth and long yellow hair was sitting on the end of it. His mother moved up beside her and left room for Julian beside herself. He sat down and looked at the floor across the aisle where a pair of thin feet in red and white canvas sandals were planted.

His mother immediately began a general conversation meant to attract anyone who felt like talking. 'Can it get any hotter?' she said and removed from her purse a folding fan, black with a Japanese scene on it, which she began to flutter before her.

'I reckon it might could,' the woman with the protruding teeth said, 'but I know for a fact my apartment couldn't get no hotter.'

143

'It must get the afternoon sun,' his mother said. She sat forward and looked up and down the bus. It was half filled. Everybody was white. 'I see we have the bus to ourselves,' she said. Julian cringed.

'For a change,' said the woman across the aisle, the owner of the red and white canvas sandals. 'I come on one the other day and they were thick as fleas – up front and all through.'

'The world is in a mess everywhere,' his mother said. 'I don't know how we've let it get in this fix.'

'What gets my goat is all those boys from good families stealing automobile tyres,' the woman with the protruding teeth said. 'I told my boy, I said you may not be rich but you been raised right and if I ever catch you in any such mess, they can send you on to the reformatory. Be exactly where you belong.'

'Training tells,' his mother said. 'Is your boy in high school?'

'Ninth grade,' the woman said.

'My son just finished college last year. He wants to write but he's selling typewriters until he gets started,' his mother said.

The woman leaned forward and peered at Julian. He threw her such a malevolent look that she subsided against the seat. On the floor across the aisle there was an abandoned newspaper. He got up and got it and opened it out in front of him. His mother discreetly continued the conversation in a lower tone but the woman across the aisle said in a loud voice, 'Well that's nice. Selling typewriters is close to writing. He can go right from one to the other.'

'I tell him,' his mother said, 'that Rome wasn't built in a day.'

Behind the newspaper Julian was withdrawing into the inner compartment of his mind where he spent most of his time. This was a kind of mental bubble in which he established himself when he could not bear to be a part of what was going on around him. From it he could see out and judge but in it he was safe from any kind of penetration from without. It was the only place where he felt free of the general idiocy of his fellows. His mother had never entered it but from it he could see her with absolute clarity.

The old lady was clever enough and he thought that if she had started from any of the right premises, more might have been expected of her. She lived according to the laws of her own fantasy world, outside of which he had never seen her set foot. The law of it was to sacrifice herself for him after she had first created the necessity to do so by making a mess of things. If he had permitted her sacrifices, it was only because her lack of foresight had made them necessary. All of her life had been a struggle to act like a Chestny without the Chestny goods, and to give him everything she thought a Chestny ought to have; but since, said she, it was fun to struggle, why complain? And when you had won, as she had won, what fun to look back on the hard times! He could not forgive her that she had enjoyed the struggle and that she thought *she* had won.

What she meant when she said she had won was that she had brought him up successfully and had sent him to college and that he had turned out so well – good looking (her teeth had gone unfilled so that his could be straightened), intelligent (he realized he was too intelligent to be a success), and with a future ahead of him (there was of course no future ahead of him). She excused his gloominess on the grounds that he was still growing up and his radical ideas on his lack of practical experience. She said he didn't yet know a thing about 'life', that he hadn't even entered the real world – when already he was as disenchanted with it as a man of fifty.

The further irony of all this was that in spite of her, he had turned out so well. In spite of going to only a third-rate college, he had, on his own initiative, come out with a first-rate education; in spite of growing up dominated by a small mind, he had ended up with a large one; in spite of all her foolish views, he was free of prejudice and unafraid to face facts. Most miraculous of all, instead of being blinded by love for her as she was for him, he had cut himself emotionally free of her and could see her with complete objectivity. He was not dominated by his mother.

The bus stopped with a sudden jerk and shook him from his meditation. A woman from the back lurched forward with little steps and barely escaped falling in his newspaper as she righted herself. She got off and a large Negro got on. Julian kept his paper lowered to watch. It gave him a certain satisfaction to see injustice in daily operation. It confirmed his view that with a few exceptions there was no one worth knowing within a radius of three hundred miles. The Negro was well dressed and carried a briefcase. He looked around and then sat down on the other end of the seat where the woman with the red and white canvas sandals was sitting. He immediately unfolded a newspaper and obscured himself behind it. Julian's mother's elbow at once prodded insistently into his ribs. 'Now you see why I won't ride on these buses by myself,' she whispered.

The woman with the red and white canvas sandals had risen at the same time the Negro sat down and had gone further back in the bus and taken the seat of the woman who had got off. His mother leaned forward and cast her an approving look.

Julian rose, crossed the aisle, and sat down in the place of the woman with the canvas sandals. From this position, he looked serenely across at his mother. Her face had turned an angry red. He stared at her, making his eyes the eyes of a stranger. He felt his tension suddenly lift as if he had openly declared war on her.

146

He would have liked to get in conversation with the Negro and to talk with him about art or politics or any subject that would be above the comprehension of those around them, but the man remained entrenched behind his paper. He was either ignoring the change of seating or had never noticed it. There was no way for Julian to convey his sympathy.

His mother kept her eyes fixed reproachfully on his face. The woman with the protruding teeth was looking at him avidly as if he were a type of monster new to her.

'Do you have a light?' he asked the Negro.

Without looking away from his paper, the man reached in his pocket and handed him a packet of matches.

'Thanks,' Julian said. For a moment he held the matches foolishly. A NO SMOKING sign looked down upon him from over the door. This alone would not have deterred him; he had no cigarettes. He had quit smoking some months before because he could not afford it. 'Sorry,' he muttered and handed back the matches. The Negro lowered the paper and gave him an annoyed look. He took the matches and raised the paper again.

His mother continued to gaze at him but she did not take advantage of his momentary discomfort. Her eyes retained their battered look. Her face seemed to be unnaturally red, as if her blood pressure had risen. Julian allowed no glimmer of sympathy to show on his face. Having got the advantage, he wanted desperately to keep it and carry it through. He would have liked to teach her a lesson that would last her a while, but there seemed no way to continue the point. The Negro refused to come out from behind his paper.

Julian folded his arms and looked stolidly before him, facing her but as if he did not see her, as if he had ceased to recognize her existence. He visualized a scene in which, the bus having reached their stop, he would remain in his seat and when she said, 'Aren't you going to get off?' he would look at her as at a stranger who had rashly addressed him. The corner they got off on was usually deserted, but it was well lighted and it would not hurt her to walk by herself the four blocks to the Y. He decided to wait until the time came and then decide whether or not he would let her get off by herself. He would have to be at the Y at ten to bring her back, but he could leave her wondering if he was going to show up. There was no reason for her to think she could always depend on him.

He retired again into the high-ceilinged room sparsely settled with large pieces of antique furniture. His soul expanded momentarily but then he became aware of his mother across from him and the vision shrivelled. He studied her coldly. Her feet in little pumps dangled like a child's and did not quite reach the floor. She was training on him an exaggerated look of reproach. He felt completely detached from her. At that moment he could with pleasure have slapped her as he would have slapped a particularly obnoxious child in his charge.

He began to imagine various unlikely ways by which he could teach her a lesson. He might make friends with some distinguished Negro professor or lawyer and bring him home to spend the evening. He would be entirely justified but her blood pressure would rise to 300. He could not push her to the extent of making her have a stroke, and moreover, he had never been successful at making any Negro friends. He had tried to strike up an acquaintance on the bus with some of the better types, with ones that looked like professors or ministers or lawyers. One morning he had sat down next to a distinguished-looking dark brown man who had answered his questions with a sonorous solemnity but who had turned out to be an undertaker. Another day he had sat down beside a cigar-smoking Negro with a diamond ring on his finger, but after a few stilted pleasantries, the Negro had rung the buzzer and risen, slipping two lottery tickets into Julian's hand as he climbed over him to leave.

He imagined his mother lying desperately ill and his being able to secure only a Negro doctor for her. He toyed with that idea for a few minutes and then dropped it for a momentary vision of himself participating as a sympathizer in a sit-in demonstration. This was possible but he did not linger with it. Instead, he approached the ultimate horror. He brought home a beautiful suspiciously Negroid woman. Prepare yourself, he said. There is nothing you can do about it. This is the woman I've chosen. She's intelligent, dignified, even good, and she's suffered and she hasn't thought it *fun*. Now persecute us, go ahead and persecute us. Drive her out of here, but remember, you're driving me too. His eyes were narrowed and through the indignation he had generated, he saw his mother across the aisle, purple-faced, shrunken to the dwarf-like proportions of her moral nature, sitting like a mummy beneath the ridiculous banner of her hat.

He was tilted out of his fantasy again as the bus stopped. The door opened with a sucking hiss and out of the dark a large, gaily dressed, sullen-looking coloured woman got on with a little boy. The child, who might have been four, had on a short plaid suit and a Tyrolean hat with a blue feather in it. Julian hoped that he would sit down beside him and that the woman would push in beside his mother. He could think of no better arrangement.

As she waited for her tokens, the woman was surveying the seating possibilities – he hoped with the idea of sitting where she was least wanted. There was something familiar-looking about her but Julian could not place what it was. She was a giant of a woman. Her face was set not only to meet opposition but to seek it out. The downward tilt of her large lower lip was like a warning sign: DON'T TAMPER WITH ME. Her bulging figure was encased in a green crêpe dress and her feet

149

overflowed in red shoes. She had on a hideous hat. A purple velvet flap came down on one side of it and stood up on the other; the rest of it was green and looked like a cushion with the stuffing out. She carried a mammoth red pocketbook that bulged throughout as if it were stuffed with rocks.

To Julian's disappointment, the little boy climbed up on the empty seat beside his mother. His mother lumped all children, black and white, into the common category, 'cute', and she thought little Negroes were on the whole cuter than little white children. She smiled at the little boy as he climbed on the seat.

Meanwhile the woman was bearing down upon the empty seat beside Julian. To his annoyance, she squeezed herself into it. He saw his mother's face change as the woman settled herself next to him and he realized with satisfaction that this was more objectionable to her than it was to him. Her face seemed almost grey and there was a look of dull recognition in her eyes, as if suddenly she had sickened at some awful confrontation. Julian saw that it was because she and the woman had, in a sense, swapped sons. Though his mother would not realize the symbolic significance of this, she would feel it. His amusement showed plainly on his face.

The woman next to him muttered something unintelligible to herself. He was conscious of a kind of bristling next to him, muted growling like that of an angry cat. He could not see anything but the red pocketbook upright on the bulging green thighs. He visualized the woman as she had stood waiting for her tokens – the ponderous figure, rising from the red shoes upward over the solid hips, the mammoth bosom, the haughty face, to the green and purple hat.

His eyes widened.

The vision of the two hats, identical, broke upon him with the radiance of a brilliant sunrise. His face was suddenly lit with joy. He could not believe that Fate had thrust upon his

150

mother such a lesson. He gave a loud chuckle so that she would look at him and see that he saw. She turned her eyes on him slowly. The blue in them seemed to have turned a bruised purple. For a moment he had an uncomfortable sense of her innocence, but it lasted only a second before principle rescued him. Justice entitled him to laugh. His grin hardened until it said to her as plainly as if he were saying aloud: your punishment exactly fits your pettiness. This should teach you a permanent lesson.

Her eyes shifted to the woman. She seemed unable to bear looking at him and to find the woman preferable. He became conscious again of the bristling presence at his side. The woman was rumbling like a volcano about to become active. His mother's mouth began to twitch slightly at one corner. With a sinking heart, he saw incipient signs of recovery on her face and realized that this was going to strike her suddenly as funny and was going to be no lesson at all. She kept her eyes on the woman and an amused smile came over her face as if the woman were a monkey that had stolen her hat. The little Negro was looking up at her with large fascinated eyes. He had been trying to attract her attention for some time.

'Carver!' the woman said suddenly. 'Come heah!'

When he saw that the spotlight was on him at last, Carver drew his feet up and turned himself toward Julian's mother and giggled.

'Carver!' the woman said. 'You heah me? Come heah!'

Carver slid down from the seat but remained squatting with his back against the base of it, his head turned slyly around toward Julian's mother, who was smiling at him. The woman reached a hand across the aisle and snatched him to her. He righted himself and hung backwards on her knees, grinning at Julian's mother. 'Isn't he cute?' Julian's mother said to the woman with the protruding teeth.

'I reckon he is,' the woman said without conviction.

The Negress yanked him upright but he eased out of her grip and shot across the aisle and scrambled, giggling wildly, on to the seat beside his love.

'I think he likes me,' Julian's mother said, and smiled at the woman. It was the smile she used when she was being particularly gracious to an inferior. Julian saw everything lost. The lesson had rolled off her like rain on a roof.

The woman stood up and yanked the little boy off the seat as if she were snatching him from contagion. Julian could feel the rage in her at having no weapon like his mother's smile. She gave the child a sharp slap across his leg. He howled once and then thrust his head into her stomach and kicked his feet against her shins. 'Behave,' she said vehemently.

The bus stopped and the Negro who had been reading the newspaper got off. The woman moved over and set the little boy down with a thump between herself and Julian. She held him firmly by the knee. In a moment he put his hands in front of his face and peeped at Julian's mother through his fingers.

'I see yoooooooo!' she said and put her hand in front of her face and peeped at him.

The woman slapped his hand down. 'Quit yo' foolishness,' she said, 'before I knock the living Jesus out of you!'

Julian was thankful that the next stop was theirs. He reached up and pulled the cord. The woman reached up and pulled it at the same time. Oh my God, he thought. He had the terrible intuition that when they got off the bus together, his mother would open her purse and give the little boy a nickel. The gesture would be as natural to her as breathing. The bus stopped and the woman got up and lunged to the front, dragging the child, who wished to stay on, after her. Julian and his mother got up and followed. As they neared the door, Julian tried to relieve her of her pocketbook.

'No,' she murmured, 'I want to give the little boy a nickel.'

'No!' Julian hissed. 'No!'

She smiled down at the child and opened her bag. The bus door opened and the woman picked him up by the arm and descended with him, hanging at her hip. Once in the street she set him down and shook him.

Julian's mother had to close her purse while she got down the bus step but as soon as her feet were on the ground, she opened it again and began to rummage inside. 'I can't find but a penny,' she whispered, 'but it looks like a new one.'

'Don't do it!' Julian said fiercely between his teeth. There was a streetlight on the corner and she hurried to get under it so that she could better see into her pocketbook. The woman was heading off rapidly down the street with the child still hanging backward on her hand.

'Oh little boy!' Julian's mother called and took a few quick steps and caught up with them just beyond the lamp-post. 'Here's a bright new penny for you,' and she held out the coin, which shone bronze in the dim light.

The huge woman turned and for a moment stood, her shoulders lifted and her face frozen with frustrated rage, and stared at Julian's mother. Then all at once she seemed to explode like a piece of machinery that had been given one ounce of pressure too much. Julian saw the black fist swing out with the red pocketbook. He shut his eyes and cringed as he heard the woman shout, 'He don't take nobody's pennies!' When he opened his eyes, the woman was disappearing down the street with the little boy staring wide-eyed over her shoulder. Julian's mother was sitting on the sidewalk.

'I told you not to do that,' Julian said angrily. 'I told you not to do that!'

He stood over her for a minute, gritting his teeth. Her legs were stretched out in front of her and her hat was on her lap. He squatted down and looked her in the face. It was totally expressionless. 'You got exactly what you deserved,' he said. 'Now get up.'

153

FLANNERY O'CONNOR

He picked up her pocketbook and put what had fallen out back in it. He picked the hat up off her lap. The penny caught his eye on the sidewalk and he picked that up and let it drop before her eyes into the purse. Then he stood up and leaned over and held his hands out to pull her up. She remained immobile. He sighed. Rising above them on either side were black apartment buildings, marked with irregular rectangles of light. At the end of the block a man came out of a door and walked off in the opposite direction. 'All right,' he said, 'suppose somebody happens by and wants to know why you're sitting on the sidewalk?'

She took the hand and, breathing hard, pulled heavily up on it and then stood for a moment, swaying slightly as if the spots of light in the darkness were circling around her. Her eyes, shadowed and confused, finally settled on his face. He did not try to conceal his irritation. 'I hope this teaches you a lesson,' he said. She leaned forward and her eyes raked his face. She seemed trying to determine his identity. Then, as if she found nothing familiar about him, she started off with a headlong movement in the wrong direction.

'Aren't you going on to the Y?' he asked.

'Home,' she muttered.

'Well, are we walking?'

For answer she kept going. Julian followed along, his hands behind him. He saw no reason to let the lesson she had had go without backing it up with an explanation of its meaning. She might as well be made to understand what had happened to her. 'Don't think that was just an uppity Negro woman,' he said. 'That was the whole coloured race which will no longer take your condescending pennies. That was your black double. She can wear the same hat as you, and to be sure,' he added gratuitously (because he thought it was funny), 'it looked better on her than it did on you. What all this means,' he said, 'is that the old world is gone. The old

154

manners are obsolete and your graciousness is not worth a damn.' He thought bitterly of the house that had been lost for him. 'You aren't who you think you are,' he said.

She continued to plough ahead, paying no attention to him. Her hair had come undone on one side. She dropped her pocketbook and took no notice. He stooped and picked it up and handed it to her but she did not take it.

'You needn't act as if the world had come to an end,' he said, 'because it hasn't. From now on you've got to live in a new world and face a few realities for a change. Buck up,' he said, 'it won't kill you.'

She was breathing fast.

'Let's wait on the bus,' he said.

'Home,' she said thickly.

'I hate to see you behave like this,' he said. 'Just like a child. I should be able to expect more of you.' He decided to stop where he was and make her stop and wait for the bus. 'I'm not going any farther,' he said, stopping. 'We're going on the bus.'

She continued to go on as if she had not heard him. He took a few steps and caught her arm and stopped her. He looked into her face and caught his breath. He was looking into a face he had never seen before. 'Tell Grandpa to come get me,' she said.

He stared, stricken.

'Tell Caroline to come get me,' she said.

Stunned, he let her go and she lurched forward again, walking as if one leg were shorter than the other. A tide of darkness seemed to be sweeping her from him. 'Mother!' he cried. 'Darling, sweetheart, wait!' Crumpling, she fell to the pavement. He dashed forward and fell at her side, crying, 'Mamma, Mamma!' He turned her over. Her face was fiercely distorted. One eye, large and staring, moved slightly to the left as if it had become unmoored. The other remained fixed on him, raked his face again, found nothing and closed.

'Wait here, wait here!' he cried and jumped up and began to run for help toward a cluster of lights he saw in the distance ahead of him. 'Help, help!' he shouted, but his voice was thin, scarcely a thread of sound. The lights drifted farther away the faster he ran and his feet moved numbly as if they carried him nowhere. The tide of darkness seemed to sweep him back to her, postponing from moment to moment his entry into the world of guilt and sorrow.

The title comes from the French Catholic theologian Teilhard de Chardin: the general sense seems to be that all the separate events which happen on this earth eventually unify (in God's knowledge?).

Most stories so far in this book are told in the first person, from a single point of view. Where third-person narration has been used it has been 'omniscient' (see notes to 'Maria'). But now we have a story told in the third person, yet restricted to a single viewpoint: we never learn the thoughts of anyone except Julian. And even when for a moment we think we are seeing him externally (second paragraph) we may simply be looking with him into the hall mirror, as he waits behind his mother. Then in the next paragraph the word 'hideous' sounds very much like Julian's own. And so, most suspiciously, does the description of him (pp. 145–146) as 'good-looking', 'intelligent', 'free of prejudice' and, most significant, 'not dominated by his mother'. This is Julian on Julian.

By not using omniscient narration, the author locks us into Julian's emotions; but by not using the first person she deceives us, at least partially, into accepting them. We would be more suspicious if he were telling the story.

The intention is to sweep us along on Julian's holier-than-thou exasperation at his mother (and many readers may some-

times have felt similarly about a parent!). We fall with him into the sin of self-righteousness. Then on the last pages, having probably shared Julian's anger at his mother's racist prejudice, and also the anger of the black woman who knocks her down, we stumble into his 'guilt and sorrow' as his mother lies (dying?) on the pavement. Along with him, though vicariously (at second hand), we learn a lesson. Finally we may stand back enough to feel compassion for him, the mother-dominated son with no future: in the last sentence the tide of darkness sweeps him back to her as to a consoling mother's arms, holding at bay the world of responsibility.

FOR FURTHER READING:

The Complete Stories of Flannery O'Connor (Faber). A strange, rich feast.

NADINE GORDIMER

★

Nadine Gordimer was born and lives in South Africa, and has been writing about her homeland through all its most difficult years. She writes with equal understanding about the power-holding heirs of white colonial settlers, the descendants of Asian traders (the characters we meet in this story) and the original ('native') black Africans. The last form the great majority of South Africans, and have also been the most disadvantaged: until recently they were expected to carry identity pass-books at all times.

A Chip of Glass Ruby

★

When the duplicating machine was brought into the house, Bamjee said, 'Isn't it enough that you've got the Indians' troubles on your back?' Mrs Bamjee said, with a smile that showed the gap of a missing tooth but was confident all the same, 'What's the difference, Yusuf? We've all got the same troubles.'

'Don't tell me that. We don't have to carry passes; let the natives protest against passes on their own, there are millions of them. Let them go ahead with it.'

The nine Bamjee and Pahad children were present at this exchange as they were always; in the small house that held them all there was no room for privacy for the discussion of matters they were too young to hear, and so they had never been too young to hear anything. Only their sister and half-sister, Girlie, was missing; she was the eldest, and married. The children looked expectantly, unalarmed and interested, at Bamjee, who had neither left the room nor settled down again to the task of rolling his own cigarettes, which had been interrupted by the arrival of the duplicator. He had looked at the thing that had come hidden in a wash-basket and conveyed in a black man's taxi, and the children turned on it too, their black eyes surrounded by thick lashes like those still, open flowers with hairy tentacles that close on whatever touches them.

'A fine thing to have on the table where we eat,' was all he said at last. They smelled the machine among them; a smell of cold black grease. He went out, heavily on tiptoe, in his troubled way.

'It's going to go nicely on the sideboard!' Mrs Bamjee was busy making a place by removing the two pink glass vases filled with plastic carnations and the hand-painted velvet runner with the picture of the Taj Mahal.

After supper she began to run off leaflets on the machine. The family lived in that room – the three other rooms in the house were full of beds – and they were all there. The older children shared a bottle of ink while they did their homework, and the two little ones pushed a couple of empty milk bottles in and out the chair legs. The three-year-old fell asleep and was carted away by one of the girls. They all drifted off to bed eventually; Bamjee himself went before the older children – he was a fruit-and-vegetable hawker and was up at half past four every morning to get to the market by five. 'Not long now,' said Mrs Bamjee. The older children looked up and smiled at him. He turned his back on her. She still wore the traditional clothing of a Moslem woman, and her body, which was scraggy and unimportant as a dress on a peg when

159

it was not host to a child, was wrapped in the trailing rags of a cheap sari and her thin black plait was greased. When she was a girl, in the Transvaal town where they lived still, her mother fixed a chip of glass ruby in her nostril; but she had abandoned that adornment as too old-style, even for her, long ago.

She was up until long after midnight, turning out leaflets. She did it as if she might have been pounding chillies.

Bamjee did not have to ask what the leaflets were. He had read the papers. All the past week Africans had been destroying their passes and then presenting themselves for arrest. Their leaders were jailed on charges of incitement, campaign offices were raided – someone must be helping the few minor leaders who were left to keep the campaign going without offices or equipment. What was it the leaflets would say – 'Don't go to work tomorrow', 'Day of Protest', 'Burn Your Pass for Freedom'? He didn't want to see.

He was used to coming home and finding his wife sitting at the table deep in discussion with strangers or people whose names were familiar by repute. Some were prominent Indians, like the lawyer, Dr Abdul Mohammed Khan, or the big businessman, Mr Moonsamy Patel, and he was flattered, in a suspicious way, to meet them in his house. As he came home from work next day he met Dr Khan coming out of the house and Dr Khan – a highly educated man – said to him, 'A wonderful woman.' But Bamjee had never caught his wife out in any presumption; she behaved properly, as any Moslem woman should, and once her business with such gentlemen was over would never, for instance, have sat down to eat with them. He found her now back in the kitchen, setting about the preparation of dinner and carrying on a conversation on several different wavelengths with the children. 'It's really a shame if you're tired of lentils, Jimmy, because that's what you're getting – Amina, hurry up, get a pot of water going – don't worry, I'll mend that in a minute, just bring the yellow cotton, and there's a needle in the cigarette box on the sideboard.'

'Was that Dr Khan leaving?' said Bamjee.

'Yes, there's going to be a stay-at-home on Monday. Desai's ill, and he's got to get the word around by himself. Bob Jali was up all last night printing leaflets, but he's gone to have a tooth out.' She had always treated Bamjee as if it were only a mannerism that made him appear uninterested in politics, the way some woman will persist in interpreting her husband's bad temper as an endearing gruffness hiding boundless goodwill, and she talked to him of these things just as she passed on to him neighbours' or family gossip.

'What for do you want to get mixed up with these killings and stonings and I don't know what? Congress should keep out of it. Isn't it enough with the Group Areas?'

She laughed. 'Now, Yusuf, you know you don't believe that. Look how you said the same thing when the Group Areas started in Natal. You said we should begin to worry when we get moved out of our own houses here in the Transvaal. And then your own mother lost her house in Noorddorp, and there you are; you saw that nobody's safe. Oh, Girlie was here this afternoon, she says Ismail's brother's engaged – that's nice, isn't it? His mother will be pleased; she was worried.'

'Why was she worried?' asked Jimmy, who was fifteen, and old enough to patronize his mother.

'Well, she wanted to see him settled. There's a party on Sunday week at Ismail's place – you'd better give me your suit to give to the cleaners tomorrow, Yusuf.'

One of the girls presented herself at once. 'I'll have nothing to wear, Ma.'

Mrs Bamjee scratched her sallow face. 'Perhaps Girlie will

lend you her pink, eh? Run over to Girlie's place now and say I say will she lend it to you.'

The sound of commonplaces often does service as security, and Bamjee, going to sit in the armchair with the shiny armrests that was wedged between the table and the sideboard, lapsed into an unthinking doze that, like all times of dreamlike ordinariness during those weeks, was filled with uneasy jerks and starts back into reality. The next morning, as soon as he got to market, he heard that Dr Khan had been arrested. But that night Mrs Bamjee sat up making a new dress for her daughter; the sight disarmed Bamjee, reassured him again, against his will, so that the resentment he had been making ready all day faded into a morose and accusing silence. Heaven knew, of course, who came and went in the house during the day. Twice in that week of riots, raids and arrests, he found black women in the house when he came home; plain ordinary native women in doeks, drinking tea. This was not a thing other Indian women would have in their homes, he thought bitterly; but then his wife was not like other people, in a way he could not put his finger on, except to say what it was not: not scandalous, not punishable, not rebellious. It was, like the attraction that had led him to marry her, Pahad's widow with five children, something he could not see clearly.

When the Special Branch knocked steadily on the door in the small hours of Thursday morning he did not wake up, for his return to consciousness was always set in his mind to half past four, and that was more than an hour away. Mrs Bamjee got up herself, struggled into Jimmy's raincoat which was hanging over a chair and went to the front door. The clock on the wall – a wedding present when she married Pahad – showed three o'clock when she snapped on the light, and she knew at once who it was on the other side of the door.

Although she was not surprised, her hands shook like a very old person's as she undid the locks and the complicated catch on the wire burglar-proofing. And then she opened the door and they were there – two coloured policemen in plain clothes. 'Zanip Bamjee?'

'Yes.'

As they talked, Bamjee woke up in the sudden terror of having overslept. Then he became conscious of men's voices. He heaved himself out of bed in the dark and went to the window, which, like the front door, was covered with a heavy mesh of thick wire against intruders from the dingy lane it looked upon. Bewildered, he appeared in the room, where the policemen were searching through a soapbox of papers beside the duplicating machine. 'Yusuf, it's for me,' Mrs Bamjee said.

At once, the snap of a trap, realization came. He stood there in an old shirt before the two policemen, and the woman was going off to prison because of the natives. 'There you are!' he shouted, standing away from her. 'That's what you've got for it. Didn't I tell you? Didn't I? That's the end of it now. That's the finish. That's what it's come to.' She listened with her head at the slightest tilt to one side, as if to ward off a blow, or in compassion.

Jimmy, Pahad's son, appeared at the door with a suitcase; two or three of the girls were behind him. 'Here, Ma, you take my green jersey.' 'I've found your clean blouse.' Bamjee had to keep moving out of their way as they helped their mother to make ready. It was like the preparation for one of the family festivals his wife made such a fuss over; wherever he put himself, they bumped into him. Even the two policemen mumbled, 'Excuse me', and pushed past into the rest of the house to continue their search. They took with them a tome that Nehru had written in prison; it had been bought from a persevering travelling salesman and kept, for years, on the

163

mantelpiece. 'Oh, don't take that, please,' Mrs Bamjee said suddenly, clinging to the arm of the man who had picked it up.

The man held it away from her.

'What does it matter, Ma?'

It was true that no one in the house had ever read it; but she said, 'It's for my children.'

'Ma, leave it.' Jimmy, who was squat and plump, looked like a merchant advising a client against a roll of silk she had set her heart on. She went into the bedroom and got dressed. When she came out in her old yellow sari with a brown coat over it, the faces of the children were behind her like faces on the platform at a railway station. They kissed her goodbye. The policemen did not hurry her, but she seemed to be in a hurry just the same.

'What am I going to do?' Bamjee accused them all.

The policemen looked away patiently.

'It'll be all right. Girlie will help. The big children can manage. And Yusuf –' The children crowded in around her; two of the younger ones had awakened and appeared, asking shrill questions.

'Come on,' said the policemen.

'I want to speak to my husband.' She broke away and came back to him, and the movement of her sari hid them from the rest of the room for a moment. His face hardened in suspicious anticipation against the request to give some message to the next fool who would take up her pamphleteering until he, too, was arrested. 'On Sunday,' she said. 'Take them on Sunday.' He did not know what she was talking about. 'The engagement party,' she whispered, low and urgent. 'They shouldn't miss it. Ismail will be offended.'

They listened to the car drive away. Jimmy bolted and barred the front door, and then at once opened it again; he put on the raincoat that his mother had taken off. 'Going to tell Girlie,' he said. The children went back to bed. Their father did not say a word to any of them; their talk, the crying of the younger ones and the argumentative voices of the older, went on in the bedrooms. He found himself alone; he felt the night all around him. And then he happened to meet the clock face and saw with a terrible sense of unfamiliarity that this was not the secret night but an hour he should have recognized: the time he always got up. He pulled on his trousers and his dirty white hawker's coat and wound his grey muffler up to the stubble on his chin and went to work.

The duplicating machine was gone from the sideboard. The policemen had taken it with them, along with the pamphlets and the conference reports and the stack of old newspapers that had collected on top of the wardrobe in the bedroom – not the thick dailies of the white men but the thin, impermanent-looking papers that spoke up, sometimes interrupted by suppression or lack of money, for the rest. It was all gone. When he had married her and moved in with her and her five children, into what had been the Pahad and became the Bamjee house, he had not recognized the humble, harmless and apparently useless routine tasks – the minutes of meetings being written up on the dining-room table at night, the government blue books that were read while the latest baby was suckled, the employment of the fingers of the older children in the fashioning of crinkle-paper Congress rosettes – as activity intended to move mountains. For years and years he had not noticed it, and now it was gone.

The house was quiet. The children kept to their lairs, crowded on the beds with the doors shut. He sat and looked at the sideboard, where the plastic carnations and the mat with the picture of the Taj Mahal were in place. For the first few weeks he never spoke of her. There was the feeling, in the house, that he had wept and raged at her, that boulders of reproach had thundered down upon her absence, and yet he had said not one word. He had not been to enquire where she was; Jimmy and Girlie had gone to Mohammed Ebrahim, the lawyer, and when he found out that their mother had been taken – when she was arrested, at least – to a prison in the next town, they had stood about outside the big prison door for hours while they waited to be told where she had been moved from there. At last they had discovered that she was fifty miles away, in Pretoria. Jimmy asked Bamjee for five shillings to help Girlie pay the train fare to Pretoria, once she had been interviewed by the police and had been given a permit to visit her mother; he put three two-shilling pieces on the table for Jimmy to pick up, and the boy, looking at him keenly, did not know whether the extra shilling meant any-thing, or whether it was merely that Bamjee had no change.

It was only when relations and neighbours came to the house that Bamjee would suddenly begin to talk. He had never been so expansive in his life as he was in the company of these visitors, many of them come on a polite call rather in the nature of a visit of condolence. 'Ah, yes, yes, you can see how I am – you see what has been done to me. Nine children, and I am on the cart all day. I get home at seven or eight. What are you to do? What can people like us do?'

'Poor Mrs Bamjee. Such a kind lady.'

'Well, you see for yourself. They walk in here in the middle of the night and leave a houseful of children. I'm out on the cart all day, I've got a living to earn.' Standing about in his shirt sleeves, he became quite animated; he would call for the girls to bring fruit drinks for the visitors. When they were gone, it was as if he, who was orthodox if not devout and never drank liquor, had been drunk and abruptly sobered up; he looked dazed and could not have gone over in his mind what he had been saying. And as he cooled, the lump of resentment and wrongedness stopped his throat again.

166

Bamjee found one of the little boys the centre of a self-important group of championing brothers and sisters in the room one evening, 'They've been cruel to Ahmed.'

'What has he done?' said the father.

'Nothing! Nothing!' The little girl stood twisting her hand-kerchief excitedly.

An older one, thin as her mother, took over, silencing the others with a gesture of her skinny hand. 'They did it at school today. They made an example of him.'

'What is an example?' said Bamjee impatiently.

'The teacher made him come up and stand in front of the whole class, and he told them, "You see this boy? His mother's in jail because she likes the natives so much. She wants the Indians to be the same as natives."'

'It's terrible,' he said. His hands fell to his sides. 'Did she ever think of this?'

'That's why Ma's *there*,' said Jimmy, putting aside his comic and emptying out his schoolbooks upon the table. 'That's all the kids need to know. Ma's there because things like this happen. Petersen's a coloured teacher, and it's his black blood that's brought him trouble all his life, I suppose. He hates anyone who says everybody's the same because that takes away from him his bit of whiteness that's all he's got. What d'you expect? It's nothing to make too much fuss about.'

'Of course, you are fifteen and you know everything,' Bamjee mumbled at him.

'I don't say that. But I know Ma, anyway.' The boy laughed.

There was a hunger strike among the political prisoners, and Bamjee could not bring himself to ask Girlie if her mother was starving herself too. He would not ask; and yet he saw in the young woman's face the gradual weakening of her mother. When the strike had gone on for nearly a week one of the elder children burst into tears at the table and could not eat. Bamjee pushed his own plate away in rage.

Sometimes he spoke out loud to himself while he was driving the vegetable lorry. 'What for?' Again and again: 'What for?' She was not a modern woman who cut her hair and wore short skirts. He had married a good plain Moslem woman who bore children and stamped her own chillies. He had a sudden vision of her at the duplicating machine, that night just before she was taken away, and he felt himself maddened, baffled and hopeless. He had become the ghost of a victim, hanging about the scene of a crime whose motive he could not understand and had not had time to learn.

The hunger strike at the prison went into the second week. Alone in the rattling cab of his lorry, he said things that he heard as if spoken by someone else, and his heart burned in fierce agreement with them. 'For a crowd of natives who'll smash our shops and kill us in our houses when their time comes.' 'She will starve herself to death there.' 'She will die there.' 'Devils who will burn and kill us.' He fell into bed each night like a stone, and dragged himself up in the mornings as a beast of burden is beaten to its feet.

One of these mornings, Girlie appeared very early, while he was wolfing bread and strong tea – alternate sensations of dry solidity and stinging heat – at the kitchen table. Her real name was Fatima, of course, but she had adopted the silly modern name along with the clothes of the young factory girls among whom she worked. She was expecting her first baby in a week or two, and her small face, her cut and curled hair and the sooty arches drawn over her eyebrows did not seem to belong to her thrust-out body under a clean smock. She wore mauve lipstick and was smiling her cocky little white girl's smile, foolish and bold, not like an Indian girl's at all.

'What's the matter?' he said.

She smiled again. 'Don't you know? I told Bobby he must get me up in time this morning. I wanted to be sure I wouldn't miss you today.'

'I don't know what you're talking about.'

She came over and put her arm up around his unwilling neck and kissed the grey bristles at the side of his mouth. 'Many happy returns! Don't you know it's your birthday?'

'No,' he said. 'I didn't know, didn't think –' He broke the pause by swiftly picking up the bread and giving his attention desperately to eating and drinking. His mouth was busy, but his eyes looked at her, intensely black. She said nothing, but stood there with him. She would not speak, and at last he said, swallowing a piece of bread that tore at his throat as it went down, 'I don't remember these things.'

The girl nodded, the Woolworth baubles in her ears swinging. 'That's the first thing she told me when I saw her yesterday – don't forget it's Bajie's birthday tomorrow.'

He shrugged over it. 'It means a lot to children. But that's how she is. Whether it's one of the old cousins or the neighbour's grandmother, she always knows when the birthday is. What importance is my birthday, while she's sitting there in a prison? I don't understand how she can do the things she does when her mind is always full of woman's nonsense at the same time – that's what I don't understand with her.'

'Oh, but don't you see?' the girl said. 'It's because she doesn't want anybody to be left out. It's because she always remembers; remembers everything – people without somewhere to live, hungry kids, boys who can't get educated – remembers all the time. That's how Ma is.'

'Nobody else is like that.' It was half a complaint.

'No, nobody else,' said his stepdaughter.

She sat herself down at the table, resting her belly. He put

169

his head in his hands. 'I'm getting old' – but he was overcome by something much more curious, by an answer. He knew why he had desired her, the ugly widow with five children; he knew what way it was in which she was not like the others; it was there, like the fact of the belly that lay between him and her daughter..

★

p. 163—Nehru was imprisoned by the British for campaigning for India's independence, and when this was eventually granted (in 1947) he became the country's first prime minister. In a serious sense Mrs Bamjee is a small part of a similar struggle, but the story balances the solemnity of this by admitting that the 'tome' (heavy book) is unread.

p. 167—'coloured' in South Africa means of mixed race, part black, part white.

p. 168—'a good plain Moslem woman who bore children and stamped her own chillies.' This points us back to the earlier comparison (p. 160) between running off leaflets and pounding chillies. Running off leaflets may seem 'masculine' (because it aims at political power, and because of the machine, smelling of grease); stamping chillies may seem traditionally 'woman's work'. But both are regular drudgery, supporting behind the scenes a world of male activity. Mrs Bamjee does things which 'old-style' women, wearing chips of glass ruby in their nostrils, were not expected to do. But she remains a carer, a provider, a rememberer of everyone's birthday.

So: what is the plot of this story? Try summarizing it, before looking at the possible answers below.

First answer: *Political resistance to an unfair regime leads to arrest and hardship, in a context of complex racism.*

Second answer: *After an upbringing which implied the subserv-*

ience of women (*symbolized by the glass ruby*), *a woman attempts to play an equal part in the 'male' world of political struggle and still retain her traditional place at the caring centre of the family.* Third answer: *a man is in love with his wife but baffled by her; at a crisis (which she has caused) he reaches towards an understanding of why he loves and married her.*

Any of these answers might be convincingly argued.

Like 'Everything That Rises Must Converge', this is third-person narrative told from only one character's viewpoint – Mr Bamjee's; but if compared the two stories reveal different effects. Here we do see some events which take place as Bamjee is asleep; and the external narrator is allowed a few generalizing comparisons (can you find them?). Also the style is confident international literary English, not at all Bamjee's: he wouldn't have said 'that the resentment he had been making ready all day faded into a morose and accusing silence.' And where Julian was self-righteous, Bamjee is baffled, which lays his story more open, inviting our opinion. Because we are less locked into Bamjee's consciousness than into Julian's, the present story feels sane, almost calm, where with Julian we go through a neurotic drama.

Like people in real life, fictional characters reveal themselves by how they look, by what they say and how they say it, and by what they do; and usually in that order. Nadine Gordimer shows us something of Mrs Bamjee immediately – the missing tooth – and more a little later. Then she lets us hear her skilful motherly control ('It's really a shame . . .' etc., p. 160). Meanwhile she has been active, turning out leaflets and cooking; but perhaps the most telling of her actions is her message from prison, to remember a birthday. Mr Bamjee is seen less externally, and is less a person of action; his character has to be gradually built up by what he says and by what we are told he feels. If in the end he seems vaguer, that may be because he is less sure of himself, but also because room is left for us to identify a little with him ourselves.

171

Nadine Gordimer

FOR FURTHER READING:

Any of Nadine Gordimer's novels or collections of stories (publishers Jonathan Cape and Penguin). Fine but quite demanding.

V. S. PRITCHETT

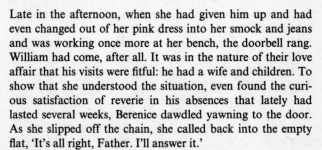

Before becoming a writer, V. S. Pritchett (born 1900) worked
in the leather trade, then as a glue salesman, then as a
journalist. He has written many kinds of book, but is particularly admired for his handling of the short story form, which
he finds 'right for the nervousness and restlessness of contemporary life'. He describes his own stories as comedies with 'a
militant, tragic edge'; and perhaps the best of comedy does
sympathize with characters at the same time as it criticizes
them. You may find your sympathies shifting about considerably in the course of this story.

A Family Man

Late in the afternoon, when she had given him up and had
even changed out of her pink dress into her smock and jeans
and was working once more at her bench, the doorbell rang.
William had come, after all. It was in the nature of their love
affair that his visits were fitful: he had a wife and children. To
show that she understood the situation, even found the curious satisfaction of reverie in his absences that lately had
lasted several weeks, Berenice dawdled yawning to the door.
As she slipped off the chain, she called back into the empty
flat, 'It's all right, Father. I'll answer it.'

William had told her to do this because she was a woman

living on her own: the call would show strangers that there was a man there to defend her. Berenice's voice was mocking, for she thought his idea possessive and ridiculous; not only that, she had been brought up by Quakers and thought it wrong to tell or act a lie. Sometimes, when she opened the door to him, she would say, 'Well! Mr Cork,' to remind him he was a married man. He had the kind of shadowed handsomeness that easily gleams with guilt, and for her this gave their affair its piquancy.

But now – when she opened the door – no William, and the yawn, its hopes and its irony, died on her mouth. A very large woman, taller than herself, filled the doorway from top to bottom, an enormous blob of pink jersey and green skirt, the jersey low and loose at the neck, a face and body inflated to the point of speechlessness. She even seemed to be asleep with her large blue eyes open.

'Yes?' said Berenice.

The woman woke up and looked unbelievingly at Berenice's feet, which were bare, for she liked to go about barefoot at home, and said, 'Is this Miss Foster's place?'

Berenice was offended by the word 'place'. 'This is Miss Foster's residence. I am she.'

'Ah,' said the woman, babyish no longer but sugary. 'I was given your address at the College. You teach at the College, I believe? I've come about the repair.'

'A repair? I make jewellery,' said Berenice. 'I do not do repairs.'

'They told me at the College you were repairing my husband's flute. I am Mrs Cork.'

Berenice's heart stopped. Her wrist went weak and her hand drooped on the door handle, and a spurt of icy air shot up her body to her face and then turned to boiling heat as it shot back again. Her head suddenly filled with chattering voices saying, Oh, God. How frightful! William, you didn't

174

tell her? Now, what are you, you, you going to do. And the word 'Do, do' clattered on in her head.

'Cork?' said Berenice. 'Flute?'

'Florence Cork,' said the woman firmly, all sleepy sweetness gone.

'Oh, yes. I am sorry. Mrs Cork. Of course, yes. Oh, do come in. I'm so sorry. We haven't met, how very nice to meet you. William's – Mr. Cork's – flute! His flute. Yes, I remember. How d'you do? How is he? He hasn't been to the College for months. Have you seen him lately – how silly, of course you have. Did you have a lovely holiday? Did the children enjoy it? I would have posted it, only I didn't know your address. Come in, please, come in.'

'In here?' said Mrs. Cork and marched into the front room where Berenice worked. Here, in the direct glare of Berenice's working lamp, Florence Cork looked even larger and even pregnant. She seemed to occupy the whole of the room as she stood in it, memorizing everything – the bench, the pots of paintbrushes, the large designs pinned to the wall, the rolls of paper, the sofa covered with papers and letters and sewing, the pink dress which Berenice had thrown over a chair. She seemed to be consuming it all, drinking all the air.

But here, in the disorder of which she was very vain, which indeed fascinated her, and represented her talent, her independence, a girl's right to a life of her own and, above all, being barefooted, helped Berenice recover her breath.

'It is such a pleasure to meet you. Mr Cork has often spoken of you to us at the College. We're quite a family there. Please sit. I'll move the dress. I was mending it.'

But Mrs Cork did not sit down. She gave a sudden lurch towards the bench, and seeing her husband's flute there propped against the wall, she grabbed it and swung it above her head as if it were a weapon.

'Yes,' said Berenice, who was thinking, Oh, dear, the

woman's drunk, 'I was working on it only this morning. I had never seen a flute like that before. Such a beautiful silver scroll. I gather it's very old, a German one, a presentation piece given to Mr Cork's father. I believe he played in a famous orchestra – where was it? – Bayreuth or Berlin? You never see a scroll like that in England, not a delicate silver scroll like that. It seems to have been dropped somewhere or have had a blow. Mr Cork told me he had played it in an orchestra himself once, Covent Garden or somewhere . . .'

She watched Mrs Cork flourish the flute in the air.

'A blow,' cried Mrs Cork, now in a rich voice. 'I'll say it did. I threw it at him.'

And then she lowered her arm and stood swaying on her legs as she confronted Berenice and said, 'Where is he?'

'Who?' said Berenice in a fright.

'My husband!' Mrs Cork shouted. 'Don't try and soft-soap me with all that twaddle. Playing in an orchestra! Is that what he has been stuffing you up with? I know what you and he are up to. He comes every Thursday. He's been here since half past two. I know. I have had this place watched.'

She swung round to the closed door of Berenice's bedroom. 'What's in there?' she shouted and advanced to it.

'Mrs. Cork,' said Berenice as calmly as she could. 'Please stop shouting. I know nothing about your husband. I don't know what you are talking about.' And she placed herself before the door of the room. 'And please stop shouting. That is my father's room.' And, excited by Mrs. Cork's accusation, she said, 'He is a very old man and he is not well. He is asleep in there.'

'In there?' said Mrs. Cork.

'Yes, in there.'

'And what about the other rooms? Who lives upstairs?'

'There are no other rooms,' said Berenice. 'I live here with my father. Upstairs? Some new people have moved in.'

Berenice was astonished by these words of hers, for she was a truthful young woman and was astonished, even excited, by a lie so vast. It seemed to glitter in the air as she spoke it.

Mrs Cork was checked. She flopped down on the chair on which Berenice had put her dress.

'My dress, if you please,' said Berenice and pulled it away.

'If you don't do it here,' said Mrs Cork, quietening and with tears in her eyes, 'you do it somewhere else.'

'I don't know anything about your husband. I only see him at the College like the other teachers. I don't know anything about him. If you will give me the flute, I will pack it up for you and I must ask you to go.'

'You can't deceive me. I know everything. You think because you are young you can do what you like,' Mrs Cork muttered to herself and began rummaging in her handbag.

For Berenice one of the attractions of William was that their meetings were erratic. The affair was like a game: she liked surprise above all. In the intervals when he was not there, the game continued for her. She liked imagining what he and his family were doing. She saw them as all glued together as if in some enduring and absurd photograph, perhaps sitting in their suburban garden, or standing beside a motor car, always in the sun, but William himself, dark-faced and busy in his gravity, a step or two back from them.

'Is your wife beautiful?' she asked him once when they were in bed.

William in his slow serious way took a long time to answer. He said at last, 'Very beautiful.'

This had made Berenice feel exceedingly beautiful herself. She saw his wife as a raven-haired, dark-eyed woman and longed to meet her. The more she imagined her, the more she felt for her, the more she saw eye to eye with her in the pleasant busy middle ground of womanish feelings and moods, for as a woman living alone she felt a firm loyalty to her sex. During this last summer when the family were on holiday she had seen them glued together again as they sat with dozens of other families in the aeroplane that was taking them abroad, so that it seemed to her that the London sky was rumbling day after day, night after night, with matrimony thirty thousand feet above the city, the countryside, the sea and its beaches where she imagined the legs of their children running across the sand, William flushed with his responsibilities, his wife turning to brown her back in the sun. Berenice was often out and about with her many friends, most of whom were married. She loved the look of harassed contentment, even the tired faces of the husbands, the alert looks of their spirited wives. Among the married she felt her singularity. She listened to their endearments and to their bickerings. She played with their children, who ran at once to her. She could not bear the young men who approached her, talking about themselves all the time, flashing with the slapdash egotism of young men trying to bring her peculiarity to an end. Among families she felt herself to be strange and necessary – a necessary secret. When William had said his wife was beautiful, she felt so beautiful herself that her bones seemed to turn to water.

But now the real Florence sat rummaging in her bag before her, this balloon-like giant, first babyish and then shouting accusations, the dreamt-of Florence vanished. This real Florence seemed unreal and incredible. And William himself changed. His good looks began to look commonplace and shady: his seriousness became furtive, his praise of her calculating. He was shorter than his wife, his face now looked hangdog, and she saw him dragging his feet as obediently he followed her. She resented that this woman had made her tell a lie, strangely intoxicating though it was to do so, and had made her feel as ugly as his wife was. For she must be, if

178

Florence was what he called 'beautiful'. And not only ugly, but pathetic and without dignity.

Berenice watched warily as the woman took a letter from her handbag.

'Then what is this necklace?' she said, blowing herself out again.

'What necklace is this?' said Berenice.

'Read it. You wrote it.'

Berenice smiled with astonishment: she knew she needed no longer defend herself. She prided herself on fastidiousness: she had never in her life written a letter to a lover – it would be like giving something of herself away, it would be almost an indecency. She certainly felt it to be very wrong to read anyone else's letters, as Mrs Cork pushed the letter at her. Berenice took it in two fingers, glanced and turned it over to see the name of the writer.

'This is not my writing,' she said. The hand was sprawling; her own was scratchy and small. 'Who is Bunny? Who is Rosie?'

Mrs Cork snatched the letter and read in a booming voice that made the words ridiculous: '"I am longing for the necklace. Tell that girl to hurry up. Do bring it next time. And darling, don't forget the flute!!! Rosie." What do you mean, who is Bunny?' Mrs Cork said. 'You know very well. Bunny is my husband.'

Berenice turned away and pointed to a small poster that was pinned to the wall. It contained a photograph of a necklace and three brooches she had shown at an exhibition in a very fashionable shop known for selling modern jewellery. At the bottom of the poster, elegantly printed, were the words

Created by Berenice

Berenice read the words aloud, reciting them as if they were a line from a poem: 'My name is Berenice,' she said.

It was strange to be speaking the truth. And it suddenly seemed to her, as she recited the words, that really William had never been to her flat, that he had never been her lover, and had never played his silly flute there, that indeed he was the most boring man at the College and that a chasm separated her from this woman, whom jealousy had made so ugly.

Mrs Cork was still swelling with unbelief, but as she studied the poster, despair settled on her face. 'I found it in his pocket,' she said helplessly.

'We all make mistakes, Mrs Cork,' Berenice said coldly across the chasm. And then, to be generous in victory, she said, 'Let me see the letter again.'

Mrs Cork gave her the letter and Berenice read it and at the word 'flute' a doubt came into her head. Her hand began to tremble and quickly she gave the letter back. 'Who gave you my address – I mean, at the College?' Berenice accused. 'There is a rule that no addresses are given. Or telephone numbers.'

'The girl,' said Mrs Cork, defending herself.

'Which girl? At Enquiries?'

'She fetched someone.'

'Who was it?' said Berenice.

'I don't know. It began with a W, I think,' said Mrs Cork.

'Wheeler?' said Berenice. 'There is a Mr Wheeler.'

'No, it wasn't a man. It was a young woman. With a W – Glowitz.'

'That begins with a G,' said Berenice.

'No,' said Mrs Cork out of her muddle, now afraid of Berenice. 'Glowitz was the name.'

'Glowitz,' said Berenice, unbelieving. 'Rosie Glowitz. She's not young.'

'I didn't notice,' said Mrs Cork. 'Is her name Rosie?'

Berenice felt giddy and cold. The chasm between herself and Mrs Cork closed up.

'Yes,' said Berenice and sat on the sofa, pushing letters and papers away from herself. She felt sick. 'Did you show her the letter?' she said.

'No,' said Mrs Cork, looking masterful again for a moment. 'She told me you were repairing the flute.'

'Please go,' Berenice wanted to say but she could not get her breath to say it. 'You have been deceived. You are accusing the wrong person. I thought your husband's name was William. He never called himself Bunny. We all called him William at the College. Rosie Glowitz wrote this letter.' But that sentence, 'Bring the flute,' was too much – she was suddenly on the side of this angry woman, she wished she could shout and break out into rage. She wanted to grab the flute that lay on Mrs Cork's lap and throw it at the wall and smash it.

'I apologize, Miss Foster,' said Mrs Cork in a surly voice. The glister of tears in her eyes, the dampness on her face, dried. 'I believe you. I have been worried out of my mind – you will understand.'

Berenice's beauty had drained away. The behaviour of one or two of her lovers had always seemed self-satisfied to her, but William, the most unlikely one, was the oddest. He would not stay in bed and gossip but he was soon out staring at the garden, looking older, as if he were travelling back into his life: then, hardly saying anything, he dressed, turning to stare at the garden again as his head came out of his shirt or he put a leg into his trousers, in a manner that made her think he had completely forgotten. Then he would go into her front room, bring back the flute and go out to the garden seat and play it. She had done a cruel caricature of him once because he looked so comical, his long lip drawn down at the mouthpiece, his eyes lowered as the thin high notes, so sad and lascivious, seemed to curl away like wisps of smoke into the trees. Sometimes she laughed, sometimes she smiled, sometimes she was touched, sometimes angry and bewildered. One proud satisfaction was that the people upstairs had complained.

She was tempted, now that she and this clumsy woman were at one, to say to her, 'Aren't men extraordinary! Is this what he does at home, does he rush out to your garden, bold as brass, to play that silly thing?' And then she was scornful. 'To think of him going round to Rosie Glowitz's and half the gardens of London doing this!'

But she could not say this, of course. And so she looked at poor Mrs Cork with triumphant sympathy. She longed to break Rosie Glowitz's neck and to think of some transcendent appeasing lie which would make Mrs Cork happy again, but the clumsy woman went on making everything worse by asking to be forgiven. She said 'I am truly sorry' and 'When I saw your work in the shop I wanted to meet you. That is really why I came. My husband has often spoken of it.'

Well, at least, Berenice thought, she can tell a lie too. Suppose I gave her everything I've got, she thought. Anything to get her to go. Berenice looked at the drawer of her bench, which was filled with beads and pieces of polished stone and crystal. She felt like getting handfuls of it and pouring it all on Mrs Cork's lap.

'Do you work only in silver?' said Mrs Cork, dabbing her eyes.

'I am,' said Berenice, 'working on something now.'

And even as she said it, because of Mrs Cork's overwhelming presence, the great appeasing lie came out of her, before she could stop herself. 'A present,' she said. 'Actually,' she said, 'we all got together at the College. A present for Rosie Glowitz. She's getting married again. I expect that is what the

182

letter is about. Mr Cork arranged it. He is very kind and thoughtful.'

She heard herself say this with wonder. Her other lies had glittered, but this one had the beauty of a newly discovered truth.

'You mean Bunny's collecting the money?' said Mrs. Cork.

'Yes,' said Berenice.

A great laugh came out of Florence Cork. 'The big spender,' she said, laughing. 'Collecting other people's money. He hasn't spent a penny on us for thirty years. And you're all giving this to that woman I talked to who has been married twice? Two wedding presents!'

Mrs Cork sighed.

'You fools. Some women get away with it. I don't know why,' said Mrs Cork, still laughing. 'But not with my Bunny,' she said proudly and as if with alarming meaning. 'He doesn't say much. He's deep, is my Bunny!'

'Would you like a cup of tea?' said Berenice politely, hoping she would say no and go.

'I think I will,' Mrs Cork said comfortably. 'I'm so glad I came to see you. And,' she added, glancing at the closed door, 'what about your father? I expect he could do with a cup.'

Mrs Cork now seemed wide awake and it was Berenice who felt dazed, drunkish and sleepy.

'I'll go and see,' she said.

In the kitchen she recovered and came back trying to laugh, saying, 'He must have gone for his little walk in the afternoon, on the quiet.'

'You have to keep an eye on them at that age,' said Mrs Cork.

They sat talking and Mrs Cork said, 'Fancy Mrs Glowitz getting married again.' And then absently, 'I cannot understand why she says "Bring the flute."'

'Well,' said Berenice agreeably, 'he played it at the College party.'

'Yes,' said Mrs Cork. 'But at a wedding, it's a bit pushy. You wouldn't think it of my Bunny, but he *is* pushing.'

They drank their tea and then Mrs Cork left. Berenice felt an enormous kiss on her face and Mrs Cork said, 'Don't be jealous of Mrs Glowitz, dear. You'll get your turn,' as she went.

Berenice put the chain on the door and went to her bedroom and lay on the bed.

How awful married people are, she thought. So public, sprawling over everyone and everything, always lying to themselves and forcing you to lie to them. She got up and looked bitterly at the empty chair under the tree at first and then she laughed at it and went off to have a bath so as to wash all those lies off her truthful body. Afterwards she rang up a couple called Brewster who told her to come round. She loved the Brewsters, so perfectly conceited as they were, in the burdens they bore. She talked her head off. The children stared at her.

'She's getting odd. She ought to get married,' Mrs Brewster said. 'I wish she wouldn't swoosh her hair around like that. She'd look better if she put it up.'

Short stories need clear beginnings and ends, and usually describe significant events: so we might well say that the plot of this story concerns Mrs Cork's intended showdown with Berenice, and the unexpected turns it takes. Real life, though, is more like a TV soap opera, without clear borders, endlessly leading from and into other complications, other plots. Pritchett seems to me here to achieve both: an entertaining story, but also a glimpse into others we'd like to know more of.

For example, we probably feel curious about William ('Bunny'), the title character who doesn't appear. And also about Rosie Glowitz. Then at the very end I find I want to know more about the Brewsters and Berenice: a whole new episode seems to be beginning. Mrs Brewster's voice, in the last words of the story, is a major shift of viewpoint: the first time we see Berenice through another character's eyes (the first time we see her hair!). In a way perhaps Mrs Brewster is answering back on behalf of all the married people on whose lives Berenice is a sort of patronizing parasite. (Or is that too hard on her?)

A good reader can think beyond the presented viewpoint, and imagine how the story might look from other positions. So, as a creative study, you might re-tell 'A Family Man' from the viewpoint of one of the other characters. This kind of speculation is part of good reading, because at any level a story has to be created by its reader as well as by its writer.

FOR FURTHER READING:

Collected Stories by V. S. Pritchett (Penguin).

BHARATI MUKHERJEE

Bharati Mukherjee was born and educated in India and later moved to the USA to study and teach. Her own experience of culture-clash seems to lie behind her vivid novels and stories.

'The American dream' is of a genuinely multicultural country where everyone would have equal rights and equal dignity. For immigrants it is traditionally symbolized by the Statue of Liberty (the Lady) on an island opposite New York harbour. A comparable dream is that of liberation, for women restricted by traditional cultures.

In the first paragraph, Panna Bhatt, the Indian narrator, is at the theatre in New York with her friend Imre. In the play (*Glengarry Glen Ross* by David Mamet) a real-estate salesman (estate agent) is being abusive about Indian immigrants, claiming it is particularly hard to sell to them. 'Patel' is a common Indian name (though the Hungarian Imre doesn't know this).

A Wife's Story

Imre says forget it, but I'm going to write David Mamet. So Patels are hard to sell real estate to. You buy them a beer, whisper *Glengarry Glen Ross*, and they smell swamp instead of sun and surf. They work hard, eat cheap, live ten to a room, stash their savings under futons in Queens, and before

186

you know it they own half of Hoboken. You say, where's the sweet gullibility that made this nation great?

Polish jokes, Patel jokes: that's not why I want to write Mamet.

Seen their women?

Everybody laughs. Imre laughs. The dozing fat man with the Barnes & Noble sack between his legs, the woman next to him, the usher, everybody. The theatre isn't so dark that they can't see me. In my red silk sari I'm conspicuous. Plump, gold paisleys sparkle on my chest.

The actor is just warming up. *Seen their women?* He plays a salesman, he's had a bad day and now he's in a Chinese restaurant trying to loosen up. His face is pink. His wool-blend slacks are creased at the crotch. We bought our tickets at half-price, we're sitting in the front row, but at the edge, and we see things we shouldn't be seeing. At least I do, or think I do. Spittle, actors goosing each other, little winks, streaks of make-up.

Maybe they're improvising dialogue too. Maybe Mamet's provided them with insult kits, Thursdays for Chinese, Wednesdays for Hispanics, today for Indians. Maybe they get together before curtain time, see an Indian woman settling in the front row off to the side, and say to each other: 'Hey, forget Friday. Let's get *her* today. See if she cries. See if she walks out.' Maybe, like the salesmen they play, they have a little bet on.

Maybe I shouldn't feel betrayed.

Their women, he goes again. *They look like they've just been fucked by a dead cat.*

The fat man hoots so hard he nudges my elbow off our shared armrest.

'Imre. I'm going home.' But Imre's hunched so far forward he doesn't hear. English isn't his best language. A refugee from Budapest, he has to listen hard. 'I didn't pay eighteen dollars to be insulted.'

I don't hate Mamet. It's the tyranny of the American dream that scares me. First, you don't exist. Then you're invisible. Then you're funny. Then you're disgusting. Insult, my American friends will tell me, is a kind of acceptance. No instant dignity here. A play like this, back home, would cause riots. Communal, racist, and antisocial. The actors wouldn't make it off stage. This play, and all these awful feelings, would be safely locked up.

I long, at times, for clear-cut answers. Offer me instant dignity, today, and I'll take it.

'What?' Imre moves toward me without taking his eyes off the actor. 'Come again?'

Tears come. I want to stand, scream, make an awful scene. I long for ugly, nasty rage.

The actor is ranting, flinging spittle. *Give me a chance. I'm not finished, I can get back on the board. I tell that asshole, give me a real lead. And what does that asshole give me? Patels. Nothing but Patels.*

This time Imre works an arm around my shoulders. 'Panna, what is Patel? Why are you taking it all so personally?'

I shrink from his touch, but I don't walk out. Expensive girls' schools in Lausanne and Bombay have trained me to behave well. My manners are exquisite, my feelings are delicate, my gestures refined, my moods undetectable. They have seen me through riots, uprootings, separation, my son's death.

'I'm not taking it personally.'

The fat man looks at us. The woman looks too, and shushes.

I stare back at the two of them. Then I stare, mean and cool, at the man's elbow. Under the bright blue polyester Hawaiian shirt sleeve, the elbow looks soft and runny. 'Excuse me,' I say. My voice has the effortless meanness of well-bred displaced Third World women, though my rhetoric has been learned elsewhere. 'You're exploiting my space.'

Startled, the man snatches his arm away from me. He cradles it against his breast. By the time he's ready with comebacks, I've turned my back on him. I've probably ruined the first act for him. I know I've ruined it for Imre.

It's not my fault; it's the *situation*. Old colonies wear down. Patels – the new pioneers – have to be suspicious. Idi Amin's lesson is permanent. AT&T wires move good advice from continent to continent. Keep all assets liquid. Get into Seven-11s, get out of condos and motels. I know how both sides feel, that's the trouble. The Patel sniffing out scams, the sad salesmen on the stage: post-colonialism has made me their referee. It's hate I long for; simple, brutish, partisan hate.

After the show Imre and I make our way toward Broadway. Sometimes he holds my hand; it doesn't mean anything more than that crazies and drunks are crouched in doorways. Imre's been here over two years, but he's stayed very old-world, very courtly, openly protective of women. I met him in a seminar on special ed. last semester. His wife is a nurse somewhere in the Hungarian countryside. There are two sons, and miles of petitions for their emigration. My husband manages a mill two hundred miles north of Bombay. There are no children.

'You make things tough on yourself,' Imre says. He assumed Patel was a Jewish name or maybe Hispanic; everything makes equal sense to him. He found the play tasteless, he worried about the effect of vulgar language on my sensitive ears. 'You have to let go a bit.' And as though to show me how to let go, he breaks away from me, bounds ahead with his head ducked tight, then dances on amazingly jerky legs. He's a Magyar, he often tells me, and deep down, he's an Asian too. I catch glimpses of it, knife-blade Attila cheekbones, despite the blondish hair. In his faded jeans and leather jacket, he's a rock video star. I watch MTV for hours in the apartment when Charity's working the evening shift at

189

Macy's. I listen to WPLJ on Charity's earphones. Why should I be ashamed? Television in India is so uplifting.

Imre stops as suddenly as he'd started. People walk around us. The summer sidewalk is full of theatregoers in seersucker suits; Imre's year-round jacket is out of place. European. Cops in twos and threes huddle, lightly tap their thighs with night sticks and smile at me with benevolence. I want to wink at them, get us all in trouble, tell them the crazy dancing man is from the Warsaw Pact. I'm too shy to break into dance on Broadway. So I hug Imre instead.

The hug takes him by surprise. He wants me to let go, but he doesn't really expect me to let go. He staggers, though I weigh no more than 104 pounds, and with him, I pitch forward slightly. Then he catches me, and we walk arm in arm to the bus stop. My husband would never dance or hug a woman on Broadway. Nor would my brothers. They aren't stuffy people, but they went to Anglican boarding schools and they have a well-developed sense of what's silly.

'Imre.' I squeeze his big, rough hand. 'I'm sorry I ruined the evening for you.'

'You did nothing of the kind.' He sounds tired. 'Let's not wait for the bus. Let's splurge and take a cab instead.'

Imre always has unexpected funds. The Network, he calls it, Class of '56.

In the back of the cab, without even trying, I feel light, almost free. Memories of Indian destitutes mix with the hordes of New York street people, and they float free, like astronauts, inside my head. I've made it. I'm making something of my life. I've left home, my husband, to get a Ph.D. in special ed. I have a multiple-entry visa and a small scholarship for two years. After that, we'll see. My mother was beaten by her mother-in-law, my grandmother, when she'd registered for French lessons at the Alliance Française. My grandmother, the eldest daughter of a rich zamindar, was illiterate.

Imre and the cabdriver talk away in Russian. I keep my eyes closed. That way I can feel the floaters better. I'll write Mamet tonight. I feel strong, reckless. Maybe I'll write Steven Spielberg too; tell him that Indians don't eat monkey brains.

We've made it. Patels must have made it. Mamet, Spielberg: they're not condescending to us. Maybe they're a little bit afraid.

Charity Chin, my roommate, is sitting on the floor drinking Chablis out of a plastic wineglass. She is five foot six, three inches taller than me, but weighs a kilo and a half less than I do. She is a 'hands' model. Orientals are supposed to have a monopoly in the hands-modelling business, she says. She had her eyes fixed eight or nine months ago and out of gratitude sleeps with her plastic surgeon every third Wednesday.

'Oh, good,' Charity says. 'I'm glad you're back early. I need to talk.'

She's been writing cheques. MCI, Con Ed, Bonwit Teller. Envelopes, already stamped and sealed, form a pyramid between her shapely, knee-socked legs. The cheque book's cover is brown plastic, grained to look like cowhide. Each time Charity flips back the cover, white geese fly over sky-coloured cheques. She makes good money, but she's extravagant. The difference adds up to this shared, rent-controlled Chelsea one-bedroom.

'All right. Talk.'

When I first moved in, she was seeing an analyst. Now she sees a nutritionist.

'Eric called. From Oregon.'

'What did he want?'

'He wants me to pay half the rent on his loft for last spring. He asked me to move back, remember? He *begged* me.'

Eric is Charity's estranged husband.

191

'What does your nutritionist say?' Eric now wears a red jumpsuit and tills the soil in Rajneeshpuram.

'You think Phil's a creep too, don't you? What else can he be when creeps are all I attract?'

Phil is a flutist with thinning hair. He's very touchy on the subject of *flautists* versus *flutists*. He's touchy on every subject, from music to books to foods to clothes. He teaches at a small college upstate, and Charity bought a used blue Datsun ('Nissan', Phil insists) last month so she could spend weekends with him. She returns every Sunday night, exhausted and exasperated. Phil and I don't have much to say to each other – he's the only musician I know; the men in my family are lawyers, engineers, or in business – but I like him. Around me, he loosens up. When he visits, he bakes us loaves of pumpernickel bread. He waxes our kitchen floor. Like many men in this country, he seems to me a displaced child, or even a woman, looking for something that passed him by, or for something that he can never have. If he thinks I'm not looking, he sneaks his hands under Charity's sweater, but there isn't too much there. Here, she's a model with high ambitions. In India, she'd be a flat-chested old maid.

I'm shy in front of the lovers. A darkness comes over me when I see them horsing around.

'It isn't the money,' Charity says. Oh? I think. 'He says he still loves me. Then he turns around and asks me for five hundred.'

What's so strange about that, I want to ask. She still loves Eric, and Eric, red jumpsuit and all, is smart enough to know it. Love is a commodity, hoarded like any other. Mamet knows. But I say, 'I'm not the person to ask about love.' Charity knows that mine was a traditional Hindu marriage. My parents, with the help of a marriage broker, who was my mother's cousin, picked out a groom. All I had to do was get to know his taste in food.

192

It'll be a long evening, I'm afraid. Charity likes to confess. I unpleat my silk sari – it no longer looks too showy – wrap it in muslin cloth and put it away in a dresser drawer. Saris are hard to have laundered in Manhattan, though there's a good man in Jackson Heights. My next step will be to brew us a pot of chrysanthemum tea. It's a very special tea from the mainland. Charity's uncle gave it to us. I like him. He's a humpbacked, awkward, terrified man. He runs a gift store on Mott Street, and though he doesn't speak much English, he seems to have done well. Once upon a time he worked for the railways in Chengdu, Szechwan Province, and during the Wuchang Uprising, he was shot at. When I'm down, when I'm lonely for my husband, when I think of our son, or when I need to be held, I think of Charity's uncle. If I hadn't left home, I'd never have heard of the Wuchang Uprising. I've broadened my horizons.

Very late that night my husband calls me from Ahmadabad, a town of textile mills north of Bombay. My husband is a vice president at Lakshmi Cotton Mills. Lakshmi is the goddess of wealth, but LCM (Priv.), Ltd., is doing poorly. Lockouts, strikes, rock-throwings. My husband lives on digitalis, which he calls the food for our *yuga* of discontent.

'We had a bad mishap at the mill today.' Then he says nothing for seconds.

The operator comes on. 'Do you have the right party, sir? We're trying to reach Mrs Butt.'

'Bhatt,' I insist. 'B for Bombay, H for Haryana, A for Ahmadabad, double T for Tamil Nadu.' It's a litany. 'This is she.'

'One of our lorries was firebombed today. Resulting in three deaths. The driver, old Karamchand, and his two children.'

I know how my husband's eyes look this minute, how the

eye rims sag and the yellow corneas shine and bulge with pain. He is not an emotional man – the Ahmadabad Institute of Management has trained him to cut losses, to look on the bright side of economic catastrophes – but tonight he's feeling low. I try to remember a driver named Karamchand, but can't. That part of my life is over, the way *trucks* have replaced *lorries* in my vocabulary, the way Charity Chin and her lurid love life have replaced inherited notions of marital duty. Tomorrow he'll come out of it. Soon he'll be eating again. He'll sleep like a baby. He's been trained to believe in turnovers. Every morning he rubs his scalp with cantharidine oil so his hair will grow back again.

'It could be your car next.' Affection, love. Who can tell the difference in a traditional marriage in which a wife still doesn't call her husband by his first name?

'No. They know I'm a flunky, just like them. Well paid, maybe. No need for undue anxiety, please.'

Then his voice breaks. He says he needs me, he misses me, he wants me to come to him damp from my evening shower, smelling of sandalwood soap, my braid decorated with jasmines.

'I need you too.'

'Not to worry, please,' he says. 'I am coming in a fortnight's time. I have already made arrangements.'

Outside my window, fire trucks whine, up Eighth Avenue. I wonder if he can hear them, what he thinks of a life like mine, led amid disorder.

'I am thinking it'll be like a honeymoon. More or less.'

When I was in college, waiting to be married, I imagined honeymoons were only for the more fashionable girls, the girls who came from slightly racy families, smoked Sobranies in the dorm lavatories and put up posters of Kabir Bedi, who was supposed to have made it as a big star in the West. My husband wants us to go to Niagara. I'm not to worry about

194

foreign exchange. He's arranged for extra dollars through the Gujarati Network, with a cousin in San Jose. And he's bought four hundred more on the black market. 'Tell me you need me. Panna, please tell me again.'

I change out of the cotton pants and shirt I've been wearing all day and put on a sari to meet my husband at JFK. I don't forget the jewellery; the marriage necklace of *mangalsutra*, gold drop earrings, heavy gold bangles. I don't wear them every day. In this borough of vice and greed, who knows when, or whom, desire will overwhelm.

My husband spots me in the crowd and waves. He has lost weight, and changed his glasses. The arm, uplifted in a cheery wave, is bony, frail, almost opalescent.

In the Carey Coach, we hold hands. He strokes my fingers one by one. 'How come you aren't wearing my mother's ring?'

'Because muggers know about Indian women,' I say. They know with us it's 24-carat. His mother's ring is showy, in ghastly taste anywhere but India: a blood-red Burma ruby set in a gold frame of floral sprays. My mother-in-law got her guru to bless the ring before I left for the States.

He looks disconcerted. He's used to a different role. He's the knowing, suspicious one in the family. He seems to be sulking, and finally he comes out with it. 'You've said nothing about my new glasses.' I compliment him on the glasses, how chic and Western-executive they make him look. But I can't help the other things, necessities until he learns the ropes. I handle the money, buy the tickets. I don't know if this makes me unhappy.

Charity drives her Nissan upstate, so for two weeks we are to have the apartment to ourselves. This is more privacy than we ever had in India. No parents, no servants, to keep us modest. We play at housekeeping. Imre has lent us a hibachi, and I grill saffron chicken breasts. My husband marvels at the size of the Perdue hens. 'They're big like peacocks, no? These Americans, they're really something!' He tries out pizzas, burgers, McNuggets. He chews. He explores. He judges. He loves it all, fears nothing, feels at home in the summer odours, the clutter of Manhattan streets. Since he thinks that the American palate is bland, he carries a bottle of red peppers in his pocket. I wheel a shopping cart down the aisles of the neighbourhood Grand Union, and he follows, swiftly, greedily. He picks up hair rinses and high-protein diet powders. There's so much I already take for granted.

One night, Imre stops by. He wants us to go with him to a movie. In his work shirt and red leather tie, he looks arty or strung out. It's only been a week, but I feel as though I am really seeing him for the first time. The yellow hair worn very short at the sides, the wide, narrow lips. He's a good-looking man, but selfconscious, almost arrogant. He's picked the movie we should see. He always tells me what to see, what to read. He buys the *Voice*. He's a natural avant-gardist. For tonight he's chosen *Numéro Deux*.

'Is it a musical?' my husband asks. The Radio City Music Hall is on his list of sights to see. He's read up on the history of the Rockettes. He doesn't catch Imre's sympathetic wink.

Guilt, shame, loyalty. I long to be ungracious, not ingratiate myself with both men.

That night my husband calculates in rupees the money we've wasted on Godard. 'That refugee fellow, Nagy, must have a screw loose in his head. I paid very steep price for dollars on the black market.'

Some afternoons we go shopping. Back home we hated shopping, but now it is a lovers' project. My husband's shopping list startles me. I feel I am just getting to know him. Maybe, like Imre, freed from the dignities of old-world culture, he too could get drunk and squirt Cheez Whiz on a guest. I watch him dart into stores in his gleaming leather shoes. Jockey shorts on sale in outdoor bins on Broadway entrance him. White tube socks with different bands of colour delight him. He looks for microcassettes, for anything small and electronic and smuggleable. He needs a garment bag. He calls it a 'wardrobe', and I have to translate.

'All of New York is having sales, no?'

My heart speeds watching him this happy. It's the third week in August, almost the end of summer, and the city smells ripe, it cannot bear more heat, more money, more energy.

'This is so smashing! The prices are so excellent!' Recklessly, my prudent husband signs away traveller's cheques. How he intends to smuggle it all back I don't dare ask. With a microwave, he calculates, we could get rid of our cook.

This has to be love, I think. Charity, Eric, Phil: they may be experts on sex. My husband doesn't chase me around the sofa, but he pushes me down on Charity's battered cushions, and the man who has never entered the kitchen of our Ahmadabad house now comes toward me with a dish tub of steamy water to massage away the pavement heat.

Ten days into his vacation my husband checks out brochures for sightseeing tours. Shortline, Grayline, Crossroads: his new vinyl briefcase is full of schedules and pamphlets. While I make pancakes out of a mix, he comparison-shops. Tour number one costs $10.95 and will give us the World Trade Center, Chinatown, and the United Nations. Tour number three would take us both uptown *and* downtown for $14.95, but my husband is absolutely sure he doesn't want to see Harlem. We settle for tour number four: downtown and the Dame. It's offered by a new tour company with a small, dirty office at 8th and 48th.

The sidewalk outside the office is colourful with tourists.
My husband sends me in to buy the tickets because he has
come to feel Americans don't understand his accent.

The dark man, Lebanese probably, behind the counter
comes on too friendly. 'Come on, doll, make my day!' He
won't say which tour is his. 'Number four? Honey, no! Look,
you've wrecked me! Say you'll change your mind.' He takes
two twenties and gives back change. He holds the tickets,
forcing me to pull. He leans closer. 'I'm off after lunch.'

My husband must have been watching me from the sidewalk. 'What was the chap saying?' he demands. 'I told you
not to wear pants. He thinks you are Puerto Rican. He thinks
he can treat you with disrespect.'

The bus is crowded and we have to sit across the aisle from
each other. The tour guide begins his patter on 46th. He
looks like an actor, his hair bleached and blow-dried. Up
close he must look middle-aged, but from where I sit his skin
is smooth and his cheeks faintly red.

'Welcome to the Big Apple, folks.' The guide uses a micro-
phone. 'Big Apple. That's what we native Manhattan degener-
ates call our city. Today we have guests from fifteen foreign
countries and six states from this US of A. That makes the
Tourist Bureau real happy. And let me assure you that while
we may be the richest city in the richest country in the world,
it's OK to tip your charming and talented attendant.' He
laughs. Then he swings his hip out into the aisle and sings a
song.

'And it's mighty fancy on old Delancey Street, you know . . .'

My husband looks irritable. The guide is, as expected, a
good singer. 'The bloody man should be giving us histories of
buildings we are passing, no?' I pat his hand, the mood
passes. He cranes his neck. Our window seats have both gone
to Japanese. It's the tour of his life. Next to this, the quick
business trips to Manchester and Glasgow pale.

'And tell me what street compares to Mott Street, in July . . .'

The guide wants applause. He manages a derisive laugh from the Americans up front. He's working the aisles now. 'I coulda been somebody, right? I coulda been a star!' Two or three of us smile, those of us who recognize the parody. He catches my smile. The sun is on his harsh, bleached hair. 'Right, your highness? Look, we gotta maharani with us! Couldn't I have been a star?'

'Right!' I say, my voice coming out a squeal. I've been trained to adapt; what else can I say?

We drive through traffic past landmark office buildings and churches. The guide flips his hands. 'Art Deco,' he keeps saying. I hear him confide to one of the Americans: 'Beats me. I went to a cheap guides' school.' My husband wants to know more about this Art Deco, but the guide sings another song.

'We made a foolish choice,' my husband grumbles. 'We are sitting in the bus only. We're not going into famous buildings.' He scrutinizes the pamphlets in his jacket pocket. I think, at least it's air-conditioned in here. I could sit here in the cool shadows of the city forever.

Only five of us appear to have opted for the 'Downtown and the Dame' tour. The others will ride back uptown past the United Nations after we've been dropped off at the pier for the ferry to the Statue of Liberty.

An elderly European pulls a camera out of his wife's designer tote bag. He takes pictures of the boats in the harbour, the Japanese in kimonos eating popcorn, scavenging pigeons, me. Then, pushing his wife ahead of him, he climbs back on the bus and waves to us. For a second I feel terribly lost. I wish we were on the bus going back to the apartment. I know I'll not be able to describe any of this to Charity, or to Imre. I'm too proud to admit I went on a guided tour.

The view of the city from the Circle Line ferry is seductive, unreal. The skyline wavers out of reach, but never quite vanishes. The summer sun pushes through fluffy clouds and dapples the glass of office towers. My husband looks thrilled, even more than he had on the shopping trips down Broadway. Tourists and dreamers, we have spent our life's savings to see this skyline, this statue.

'Quick, take a picture of me!' my husband yells as he moves toward a gap of railings. A Japanese matron has given up her position in order to change film. 'Before the Twin Towers disappear!'

I focus, I wait for a large Oriental family to walk out of my range. My husband holds his pose tight against the railing. He wants to look relaxed, an international businessman at home in all the financial markets.

A bearded man slides across the bench toward me. 'Like this,' he says and helps me get my husband in focus. 'You want me to take the photo for you?' His name, he says, is Goran. He is Goran from Yugoslavia, as though that were enough for tracking him down. Imre from Hungary, Panna from India. He pulls the old Leica out of my hand, signalling the Orientals to beat it, and clicks away. 'I'm a photographer,' he says. He could have been a camera thief. That's what my husband would have assumed. Somehow, I trusted. 'Get you a beer?' he asks.

'I don't. Drink, I mean. Thank you very much.' I say those last words very loud, for everyone's benefit. The odd bottles of Soave with Imre don't count.

'Too bad.' Goran gives back the camera.

'Take one more!' my husband shouts from the railing. 'Just to be sure!'

The island itself disappoints. The Lady has brutal scaffolding holding her in. The museum is closed. The snack bar is dirty

and expensive. My husband reads out the prices to me. He
orders two french fries and two Cokes. We sit at picnic tables
and wait for the ferry to take us back.

'What was that hippie chap saying?'

As if I could say. A day-care centre has brought its kids, at
least forty of them, to the island for the day. The kids, all
wearing name tags, run around us. I can't help noticing how
many are Indian. Even a Patel, probably a Bhatt if I looked
hard enough. They toss hamburger bits at pigeons. They kick
styrofoam cups. The pigeons are slow, greedy, persistent. I
have to shoo one off the table top. I don't think my husband
thinks about our son.

'What hippie?'

'The one on the boat. With the beard and the hair.'

My husband doesn't look at me. He shakes out his paper
napkin and tries to protect his french fries from pigeon feathers.

'Oh, him. He said he was from Dubrovnik.' It isn't true,
but I don't want trouble.

'What did he say about Dubrovnik?'

I know enough about Dubrovnik to get by. Imre's told me
about it. And about Mostar and Zagreb. In Mostar white
Muslims sing the call to prayer. I would like to see that
before I die: white Muslims. Whole peoples have moved
before me; they've adapted. The night Imre told me about
Mostar was also the night I saw my first snow in Manhattan.
We'd walked down to Chelsea from Columbia. We'd walked
and talked and I hadn't felt tired at all.

'You're too innocent,' my husband says. He reaches for my
hand. 'Panna,' he cries with pain in his voice, and I am
brought back from perfect, floating memories of snow, 'I've
come to take you back. I have seen how men watch you.'

'What?'

'Come back, now. I have tickets. We have all the things we
will ever need. I can't live without you.'

A little girl with wiry braids kicks a bottle cap at his shoes. The pigeons wheel and scuttle around us. My husband covers his fries with spread-out fingers. 'No kicking,' he tells the girl. Her name, Beulah, is printed in green ink on a heart-shaped name tag. He forces a smile, and Beulah smiles back. Then she starts to flap her arms. She flaps, she hops. The pigeons go crazy for fries and scraps.

'Special ed. course is two years,' I remind him. 'I can't go back.'

My husband picks up our trays and throws them into the garbage before I can stop him. He's carried disposability a little too far. 'We've been taken,' he says, moving toward the dock, though the ferry will not arrive for another twenty minutes. 'The ferry costs only two dollars round-trip per person. We should have chosen tour number one for $10.95 instead of tour number four for $14.95.'

With my Lebanese friend, I think. 'But this way we don't have to worry about cabs. The bus will pick us up at the pier and take us back to midtown. Then we can walk home.'

'New York is full of cheats and whatnot. Just like Bombay.' He is not accusing me of infidelity. I feel dread all the same.

That night, after we've gone to bed, the phone rings. My husband listens, then hands the phone to me. 'What is this woman saying?' He turns on the pink Macy's lamp by the bed. 'I am not understanding these Negro people's accents.'

The operator repeats the message. It's a cable from one of the directors of Lakshmi Cotton Mills. 'Massive violent labour confrontation anticipated. Stop. Return posthaste. Stop. Cable flight details. Signed Kantilal Shah.'

'It's not your factory,' I say. 'You're supposed to be on vacation.'

'So, you are worrying about me? Yes? You reject my heartfelt wishes but you worry about me?' He pulls me close, slips the straps of my nightdress off my shoulder. 'Wait a minute.'

I wait, unclothed, for my husband to come back to me. The water is running in the bathroom. In the ten days he has been here he has learned American rites: deodorants, fragrances. Tomorrow morning he'll call Air India; tomorrow evening he'll be on his way back to Bombay. Tonight I should make up to him for my years away, the gutted trucks, the degree I'll never use in India. I want to pretend with him that nothing has changed.

In the mirror that hangs on the bathroom door, I watch my naked body turn, the breasts, the thighs glow. The body's beauty amazes. I stand here shameless, in ways he has never seen me. I am free, afloat, watching somebody else.

Panna's narrative style is dry, tight-lipped, in a way very flip-American: perhaps only in the final paragraph does it begin to flow. So we must be alert for any information she lets slip, both about facts and about her feelings. She has been trained in restraint ('to behave well') – in India, where her marriage was arranged for her and 'all I had to do was get to know his taste in food'; and in expensive girls' schools in India and Europe. Consider how many potential novels are compressed, with terrible elegance, into

> *My manners are exquisite, my feelings are delicate, my gestures refined, my moods undetectable. They have seen me through riots, uprootings, separation, my son's death.*

Part of the plot of her story, then, is her allowing herself to feel freer, in America. She is still too shy to dance on Broadway, but she feels mischievous, hugs Imre, and in the cab feels 'light, almost free'. She watches American television greedily, and studs her narrative with the names of shops and brands, as if to show how well she is adjusting. And at the very end 'I am free' (triumphant?) but 'watching somebody else' (alienated from her 'self'?).

Here the American dream is almost parodied, as nearly every character we meet is of a different nationality. But early on Panna refers to the 'tyranny' of the dream (p. 188), and we note that the Lady seems to need repair, being fenced in by 'brutal scaffolding'.

Even more we see how the other dream, of 'liberation' for a woman from a patriarchal culture, can be agonizing. 'I'm not the person to ask about love,' says Panna to Charity. Well: is she or isn't she? – study all the occasions that she mentions her husband. In New York, where the gap between them might be expected to be widest, their marriage deepens, because they are both freer – he to come into her kitchen, she to view him as a person rather than lord-and-master: 'I feel I am just getting to know him.' See particularly the paragraph (p. 197) beginning 'This has to be love, I think.'

Does this 'wife's story' speak only for the bride of an arranged marriage? Or might much of it be significant for any wife? And husband?

The first-person viewpoint is essential to this story: an omniscient narrator, advising us what to think, would destroy the passion, the acuteness, the agony of Panna's dilemma. Her uncertainty, as she tries moment by moment to tell the truth of her feelings, is additionally expressed by the choice of the present tense. That tense implies no knowledge of the ultimate outcome, and we have met it previously in this collection only in trapped characters – the speaker in 'A Telephone Call', the postcard-writer in 'Having a Wonderful Time'. The question in this case is whether Panna is trapped or not; and ultimately whether, by deciding to go back to India with her husband, she might freely choose to give up freedom.

What do you think she will do? What do you want her to do?

FOR FURTHER READING:

The Middleman and Other Stories; and the novel *Jasmine*; both by Bharati Mukherjee and published by Virago.

STUDY TOPICS

———————————— ★ ————————————

These suggestions assume you have read most or all of the stories in the book, and are now ready to make comparisons.

HUMOUR

'There's nothing funnier than unhappiness' says a character in Samuel Beckett's play *Endgame*. Most comedy deals with situations of potential pain. A story as light as 'Dale', for example, is full of such situations.

Study the humour in several stories. Is it cruel? compassionate? indifferent? How much does it depend on skilful phrasing? (a question also about Style).

GUILT

In a number of these stories we see the central characters feeling guilt, or trying to deny that they feel it. Compare their different ways of dealing with it, in two or more stories: you might look at 'The Bewitched Jacket', 'A Telephone Call', 'Order on the Cheap', 'Everything That Rises Must Converge' or 'A Family Man'.

Study Topics

LOVE

We can argue for ever about what is 'true love'; but we are
certainly asked to accept its existence in 'Telling Stories' or
'A Letter to my Son'. Do we recognize it in the seedling
emotions of Dale and Carla? Or in the experienced Berenice
('A Family Man')? Or in the misery of 'A Telephone Call'?
What about the marriages of Mr Bamjee in 'A Chip of Glass
Ruby' or Panna Bhatt in 'A Wife's Story' (who says 'I'm not
the person to ask about love.')? Choose two or three stories
and consider how they present relationships which may or
may not be 'love'.

MALE POWER, FEMALE POWER

All Colby's so-called 'friends' seem to be male; might a
woman have made a difference? Is it significant that the
scientist's family in 'Order on the Cheap' is 'away in the
mountains'? The narrator of 'The Bewitched Jacket' has a
maid and, when he is wealthy, 'the company of marvellous
women' – but no partner. William in 'A Family Man' might
win an award for male misconduct. And of course the education of Maria, and of Mrs Bamjee and Panna Bhatt, steered
women away from public power.

Only Mrs Bamjee, in this collection, attempts to enter that
male arena. Yet many of the stories show women manipulat-
ing events unobtrusively (consider 'Telling Stories', 'Maria',
'The Writer in the Family' and 'A Wife's Story', and the
emotional domination in 'Everything That Rises Must Converge').

Compare the different presentations of male and female

power in two or more stories. Could it be significant that here female power seems sometimes to overlap with 'love'?

RACISM

Racial hostility is partly about fear of the unfamiliar and partly about defending the interests of a cultural group: either way, it expresses insecurity. Compare the part it plays in the plots of 'Everything That Rises Must Converge', 'A Chip of Glass Ruby' and 'A Wife's Story.'

PLOT

The best plots seem to grow inevitably from previous events. This can include a certain character (Maria, for example) arriving in a certain situation: clearly, with Maria stuck at the Doseleys (what a name!), something has to give. The plot of 'A Letter to Our Son' is equally specific: these particular people falling in love and making a child at this particular time in their lives – and then faced with the great fear of cancer.

In 'The Surest Thing in Show Business', a controlled situation of life-threatening risk is broken open (literally – the snakes all over the stage) by a man who is either unaware of or indifferent to that risk. We never find out which it is; and to that extent the plot is unresolved, though he has survived the immediate danger. Plotting is partly about getting characters into interesting situations – which can be hard enough; but getting them out is harder still. Maria's letter blown overboard (p. 63) doesn't seem to me to grow out of the story, as do Jonathan's final letter (p. 80) or the collapse of Julian's mother (p. 155). Berenice's inspired lie (p. 182) seems to me a particularly fine twist of plot: it gets her out of this

STUDY TOPICS

story safely, and both her lie and Mrs Cork's acceptance of it seem consistent with their characters.

Analyse the plot-structure of several stories, and consider which seem the most effective in making event grow out of character and situation.

CHARACTERIZATION

Choose two or three characters, from different stories, who seem vividly created, so that you can imagine meeting them; then study how you get to know them (the notes on p. 171 may help). You can include minor characters who appear only briefly, provided you find them convincing: a skilful writer can bring someone to life in a line or two (e.g. Miss Falconer in 'Dale', p. 28) – or sometimes it's enough to give us the outline for our own imagination (e.g. Mark Hastings, Diana's 'handsome cavalier' in 'Having a Wonderful Time', p. 42).

Many of these stories are told from inside one character's head. How do we find out what such first-person narrators – or Julian in 'Everything That Rises Must Converge' – look and sound like? Are they sometimes less clear to us than the people they meet and see externally? Perhaps that may even be an advantage, if we are meant to identify with them.

STYLE (and TONE)

Here, be cautious about the two American-translated stories ('The Bewitched Jacket' and 'Order on the Cheap'), unless you can read them in the original Italian. Elsewhere, consider the choices the writers have made, and why. One way to do this is to try rewriting one story in the style of another – an exercise which can amuse, yet soon feel like vandalism.

STUDY TOPICS

Then study the language, comparisons and tone of two or three stories which offer interesting contrasts.

SETTING

In most modern fiction, especially short stories, settings are sketched only briefly. Any details must earn their place by increasing our understanding, creating a mood, or offering a symbol (such as the Statue of Liberty imprisoned in scaffolding). From two or three stories, study how the external world is presented to us, preferably in contrasting ways with contrasting intentions.

VIEWPOINT

This is the single most important choice, for a fiction writer. The notes on pp. 64 and 156 focus on different narrative options, and on p. 185 I suggest that really good reading can involve mentally retelling the story to ourselves in other ways, from other angles.

Enjoy the narrative we're given; but question it as well. Since 'A Letter to Our Son' is a true story about real people, it may be too impertinent to wonder how Alison views it. But we can at least speculate how Andrew, after many years of marriage, would tell the story of his wedding; or how William Cork views his life; or, of course, what are the thoughts of the guy who is busy not making the awaited 'Telephone Call'. As for Colby's view . . .

Any story here is worth considering. Compare two or three of them, including at least one told in the first person and one told in the third. And always ask: what decided the writer to tell it from this angle?

ACKNOWLEDGEMENTS

──────────── ★ ────────────

I am grateful to John Adams and Rob Oliver, who introduced me to two of the stories collected here, and to John Law for other suggestions.

Acknowledgements are due to the following for permission to include stories in this anthology: the author, Carcanet Press and Arnold Mondadori Editore for 'The Bewitched Jacket' from *Restless Nights* by Dino Buzzati; Gerald Duckworth & Co and Viking Penguin for 'A Telephone Call' from *The Penguin Dorothy Parker*; the author and Christine Green for 'Telling Stories' by Maeve Binchy; the author and A P Watt Ltd for 'Dale' from *Leaving Home* by Garrison Keillor; the author c/o Margaret Hanbury for 'Having a Wonderful Time' from *Myths of the Near Future* published by Jonathan Cape and Paladin; the Literary Executors of the Estate, Jonathan Cape and Alfred A. Knopf for 'Maria' from *The Collected Stories of Elizabeth Bowen*; the author and Penguin Books Ltd for 'The Writer in the Family' from *Lives of the Poets* (Michael Joseph 1984); Aitken & Stone for 'The Surest Thing in Show Business' from *Fishes, Birds and Sons of Men* by Jesse Hill Ford; Penguin Books Limited, Summil Books and Giulio Einaudi Editore for 'Order on the Cheap' from *The Sixth Day* (Michael Joseph 1990) by Primo Levi; the author, Secker & Warburg, Rogers, Coleridge and White Ltd and G. P. Putnam's Sons for 'Some of Us Had Been Threatening Our Friend Colby' from *Forty Stories* by Donald Barthelme; the author c/o Rogers, Coleridge and White Ltd for 'A Letter to Our Son' by Peter Carey; Peters
211

Acknowledgements

Fraser & Dunlop for 'Everything that Rises Must Converge' from *The Complete Stories of Flannery O'Connor*; the author and Jonathan Cape Ltd for 'A Chip of Glass Ruby' from *Selected Stories* by Nadine Gordimer; Peters Fraser & Dunlop for 'A Family Man' from *Collected Stories* (Chatto) by V. S. Pritchett; the author and Virago Press for 'A Wife's Story' by Bharati Mukherjee.